FACES OF THE DEAD

FACES OF THE DEAD

SUZANNE WEYN

SCHOLASTIC PRESS / NEW YORK

Library of Congress Cataloging-in-Publication Data available

ISBN 978-0-545-42531-5

10 9 8 7 6 5 4 3 2 1   14 15 16 17 18

Printed in the U.S.A.   23
First edition, September 2014

The text type was set in Calisto MT.
Book design by Elizabeth B. Parisi

ℐNTRODUCTION

*C*hild of France! That is the title I am born to. It's a most fitting label.

Though at seventeen I hardly qualify as a child anymore. Still, I am my country's creation as much — perhaps even more so — as I am the offspring of my mother, Queen Marie-Antoinette, and my father, King Louis the Sixteenth. My parents created me from flesh and blood, but so has France and its Revolution molded, shaped, and twisted me into my current form. They've taken the softness that was inside and fired it into a hard shell. They have warped my once-trusting mind so that I see plots and traitors at every turn. France, I am most truly the cynical, angry, anxious child you've made me.

But it wasn't always so. There was a time when I was very different.

PART 1

MARIE-THÉRÈSE-CHARLOTTE, ROYAL CHILD OF FRANCE

CHAPTER 1

*H*ere is my first memory. I am five and Mama's smooth hand enfolds mine. She stands beside Papa, while our governess holds my little brother, Louis-Joseph. Our breath clouds up before us, but we're not cold because we are wrapped in ermine-lined cloaks. I love the softness against my cheek.

My family and I stand in front of the palace at Versailles in the minister's courtyard, encircled by the Swiss guard, our private security force. We are *among* people — not on some high-up balcony — and this has never happened to me before.

I love the smell and sounds of the crowd. All kinds of people are here. Some are very well dressed. Others are ragged and without coats or cloaks on this frigid day. But all are happy. Excited.

This mass of people is what interests me the most. The crowd is enormous. Huge! It spills out from the rings of courtyards as far as I can see. I wouldn't have ever imagined that so many people even existed.

"People have come all the way from Paris just to witness this," my father remarks to my mother.

"Such numbers," she murmurs, her eyes narrowing thoughtfully as she takes in the crowd, her royal subjects. Worry flickers across her face. Why fret on such a festive occasion? It puzzles me.

"Shall we invite them all back for a feast afterward?" I suggest, thinking that she might be concerned with the matter of how they will eat. "Wouldn't that be fun?"

"Do you think the palace is big enough to hold them all?" Mama asks with a soft smile.

"Of course it is," I say. "It's the biggest place on earth! Isn't it?"

"It must surely be one of the largest," she agrees, nodding, "but, even so, not large enough for such a multitude as this. At least I don't think so."

"Please, Mama," I beg, "these people are our subjects, aren't they? Isn't it our duty to feed them?"

Mama hugs me to her, rubbing my back. "My Mousseline Serieuse." That's her nickname for me. It means "serious muslin." She explained to me once that muslin is a fabric that appears quite dainty and delicate but is actually very strong and sturdy. She says I'm like that.

Suddenly with one voice, a single awestruck breath, the crowd gasps, then coos in awe. *Ah!*

Mama squeezes my hand, and I follow her gaze into the vastness of the cornflower-blue sky. An enormous azure-blue hot air balloon floats across the billowing clouds. It's decorated with a golden fleur-de-lis, the royal symbol of my family, the Bourbons. Below the balloon hangs an open vessel that reminds me of a wooden bathtub. I can barely make out the figures of the two men standing in it. They are so high that they look like dolls in an open case.

Around me, everyone murmurs. *How wonderful! How beautiful! What heroes!*

"They've floated here all the way from the Tuileries Gardens," Mama tells me. "This has never been done before."

I gaze up into her lovely blue eyes and can see the light of excitement in them. Her mounds of blonde curls are done up even higher than usual in honor of the event. A miniature version of the hot air balloon sits at the top of her coif. It seems playful and modest compared to the tiny, many-masted ship she wore in her hair last week in homage to France's most recent naval victory at sea.

"How will they get down?" I ask.

Papa hears me. Turning, he smiles. "Watch, Marie-Thérèse," he says. "You'll see. We are entering a remarkable new era of science."

Around me, the onlookers are ecstatic or terrified. Many appear to be a little of both. A woman faints. A grown man shields his eyes as though afraid he will be blinded by the beauty of the balloon.

The hot air balloon is fascinating, but it is not what I am watching. Instead, I observe the crowd as *they* observe the balloon. I have an urge to break from my mama's grip and disappear into the field of people, become one with them. I wouldn't dare, of course. But still, I long for the warmth of the French people. My people.

I observe the children laughing and playing, picnicking with their families on the lawn. How I envy them — their freedom.

What would it be like? I wonder.

CHAPTER 2

I am fifteen and this is my passion: to dance! The stiff minuets and cotillions danced at court functions are interesting to watch, but they're not what I love. When there is a lively gavotte and the men spin the women, I would die to join in. I'm too young, of course. But someday soon . . .

At Mama's country house that lies far out on the Versailles property, I can dance as I like. At her rustic refuge I can jig and jump and spin until I am dizzy and spent. Sometimes Mama's royal friends join me; other times they play cards and gamble, recite poetry so dramatic that Mama sometimes weeps, and perform comical plays that make her roll with laughter.

When Mama is at her country house, she's not at all queenly. I am happiest there with her because *she* is happiest there: smiling and humming country songs from her girlhood home in Austria. She says it was lovely and relaxed there, not at all like the stiff formality here at Versailles. She's sad that she had to leave it all behind when she came to France to marry my father. Mama was thirteen when she left Austria!

At the Petit Trianon, which is the name of the country estate, I can relax, too, and just be a girl — not a princess. At the Trianon

I am only my mother and father's child — not the Child of France. There are goats to milk and fields to run in. Mama and I pretend that we are shepherdesses watching our flock.

I have a lovely music box Mama gave to me. In it are a mother and her daughter dressed as shepherdesses with straw bonnets and white gowns, and each of them carries a crook. A little lamb frolics beside them. When I wind the box, a sweet folk song plays and the mother and daughter turn.

At the country house, I also dance with Ernestine, my very dearest friend from the palace. We are only six months apart in age. Though her mother is a chambermaid, Mama took a liking to Ernestine when we were both very little and has had her come every day since then to be my companion.

When Ernestine and I are not jigging or pretending to dance in a ballet, leaping in a field, we practice court dances at the country house's party room. We twirl and curtsy, laughing and imagining all the handsome courtiers we'll someday dance with. We give up on ever mastering the longways dances, in which men and women face each other in a line, then change places and dance with different partners. The steps are monstrously confusing.

Madame Bertin, the royal wardrobe mistress, makes Ernestine and me dresses of soft white ruffled muslin similar to the one Mama likes to wear. They have wide blue sashes at the waist and matching ribbons just below the elbows. The frocks are called *gaulles* and are deliciously airy — so unlike the formal dresses that we must wear at court, with their itchy ruffled collars, tight-fitting bodices, and wide pannier hoops underneath the full skirts.

That summer Mama wears her light frock with a wide-brimmed straw bonnet adorned with fluffy blue plumed feathers. We don't wear bonnets but simply bundle our blonde curls in a blue ribbon. Our hair color is nearly the same light yellow. Only the three of us realize that Ernestine's face is framed with a more golden shade of blonde; for everyone else it's too small a detail.

How beautiful we feel as we stand side by side admiring ourselves in an oval mirror. "We're princesses disguised as country maidens," I proclaim.

"But I'm not really a princess," Ernestine says after a while.

"It doesn't matter," I reply.

CHAPTER 3

By sixteen, we've been playing the game of switching identities for years. The first time it happened, Ernestine was twelve and I was eleven and a half.

"You've been bad!" Ernestine scolded playfully on that day as she entered my bedroom.

I turned from the romance novel I'd been reading as I sprawled across my bed. "I have?"

"Yes! You were supposed to be at the queen's side when she presented twenty pounds of flour to the Ladies Orphanage Society this afternoon."

My hands flew to my cheeks as they reddened. "I completely forgot! Why didn't someone come to get me?"

"One of your mother's ladies did come, but she thought I was you. I didn't know where you were, so I went, instead."

"She couldn't tell it wasn't me?" I asked, surprised. I knew that everyone remarked how much Ernestine and I look alike, but that was the first time she'd been mistaken for me.

Ernestine shook her head.

"Mama couldn't even tell?"

"I think maybe she could."

"Why do you think that?"

Ernestine smiled. "She winked at me as I left."

"Thank you for standing in for me," I said.

"It was fun. I liked it."

That's when the idea was born. How many other royal duties could I escape with a twin who enjoyed taking my place? How much freedom could I enjoy by pretending to be her?

That's how it all begins. Ernestine sits in for me at royal events, such as stuffy dinners with visiting royalty, boring operas performed in the ballrooms, and endless speeches about enhancing the French roadways that Papa expects our whole family to attend. Ernestine claims to love it all. "Some of it is dull," she admits, "but it's such fun to be a princess if only for a few hours."

For my part, it's a chance to have some real fun. Mama provides Ernestine with lovely dresses, but they're not as grand as the ones I'm expected to wear. It's such a relief to slip into one of Ernestine's gowns and roam the palace.

On one of my roams, I persuaded a maid to teach me a jig. On another, one of the bakers taught me to make dough and shape it into a pie crust. On one beautiful day I played a game of tag with the children of the servants. It's such fun to lift my skirts and run as I could never do as a princess.

*　　*　　*

We are playing our switch game when something interesting happens. Ernestine's acting as me and attending a lecture on French horticultural advances with the rest of my family. I am running through one of the palace's many secret passageways in her dress and flat velvet shoes until I come to a door that I know well. It leads to a closet in the servants' quarters.

Pushing it forward carefully, I step into a space filled with buckets, mops, and brooms. They clatter and I hold my breath in alarm, but no one comes to investigate the noise.

Cracking open the outer door leading into the hallway, I wait for a moment to be certain that the hall is empty, and then I step out. I breathe a short sigh of relief and start to wander down the hall and around the first corner. "Good evening, Ernestine," I am greeted by a servant, a young man.

"Good evening!" I chirp back brightly, pleased that he did not bow formally to me but greeted me with friendliness. He simply assumes I belong here.

Oh, what freedom! How I love it!

"My, how those curls bounce!" says a fat maid. I smile at her and keep moving dancingly along.

Wonderful smells pull me toward the kitchen. A burly baker, the same one who taught me to make pie dough, withdraws a paddle laden with tart crusts from the stone oven. My mouth waters even though I have already dined on roasted pheasant and potatoes and feasted on strawberry custard tarts for dessert. Several maids and two footmen sit at a long plank table eating what looks like some kind of bird. Maybe it is what is left of the pheasant.

The baker smiles when he notices me. "Ernestine!" he cries happily. "So good to see you again. I have been waiting for you to escape Madame Royale and come back here where you belong. Sit! I am making a second batch of tarts. One of them will be just for you."

"Thank you. But I have already had one with Marie-Thérèse," I say. This is true.

"Have another," the baker offers with a laugh as he ladles chopped strawberries from a bowl into the tart crust. "You are too skinny."

Thanking him, I take a place at the plank table. Only after I am seated do I realize that I am across from a woman who comes to the palace to give art lessons to my aunt, Madame Élisabeth, Papa's sister.

In the art room, they fashion figures of famous people out of warm wax. Aunt Élisabeth's work is lumpy and misshapen. But the art teacher's sculptures are amazing. In the corner of the art room stands a life-size sculpture of the famous American Thomas Jefferson, whom we French admire so much. The afternoon when I peeked into the door to watch them work, I thought that the great Jefferson was really there in person until I realized he was too still to be alive. I jumped away from the door when the art teacher turned abruptly and locked me in her steely gaze.

Later, I asked Aunt Élisabeth about her and discovered that the art teacher is named Anna Marie Grosholtz. "She's Alsatian," my aunt told me. "They are more German than French over there, even though it's French territory."

Now I am sitting across the table from Mademoiselle Grosholtz. Something about her unsettles me. Perhaps it is her unsmiling face or her dark, bird-quick alertness.

She is plain, though not ugly, with brown curls tucked into a ruffled lace cap. At her neck she wears a pinned scarf over a brown gown. The rest of her is hidden under an artist's smock that is smeared with grayish wax.

As she sits with the dishes from her meal still in front of her, Mademoiselle Grosholtz works on something that she holds just beneath the table. Knitting? Needlework? I don't have the nerve to look down to see. From time to time she gazes up from her work, stares at me, and then returns to it.

Does she live here at the palace? So very many people live here in one or another of the numerous wings and buildings. It's almost impossible to know who belongs and who doesn't.

Mademoiselle Grosholtz stands, and as she does, she tosses a small beige pebble at me. Reflexively, my hand shoots up to snap it from the air. Surprised at its smooth softness, I unfold my fingers.

It is no pebble.

I hold in my hand what resembles the head of a small doll. But it is soft, still malleable. And it has been pressed with her fingers and sculpted with her fingernails.

It is an exact image of me.

How did she do it so quickly and with such accuracy? It's spooky and I don't like it. I don't like her, I decide. She scares me.

My hand curls into a fist and with a quick thump I smash the wax visage flat onto the table. Instantly, heat jumps into my face, my cheeks burning.

Mademoiselle Grosholtz laughs at me, but only with her eyes, and then walks off. She is yards away before I hear her actually chuckle.

Gazing down at the smashed wax, I regret my impulsivity. Why did it make me so uneasy that I had to destroy it?

CHAPTER 4

*T*he first time I decide that I might leave the palace dressed as Ernestine, we are sixteen.

"You're not serious?" Ernestine asks me, shocked. "You can't do that!"

We're standing in the sparkling Hall of Mirrors. The entire corridor shimmers with light as the afternoon rays come from the long outside windows and bounce off the mirrors on the other side. Crystal chandeliers throw rainbows everywhere.

"Look at us," I say, drawing her beside me, to gaze into a mirror. "Each day we look more and more alike."

"You have a better nose," Ernestine says.

"I do not," I say. "We could be twins!"

I lower my voice as two noblemen pass us, heads together, deep in murmured conversation. "I want to leave the palace dressed as you," I whisper again when they've gone by. "Please say you'll switch with me."

"But why?" Ernestine asks in exasperation. "You have everything here at the palace. No one in all of France has a more elegant, serene life than you do."

"You don't understand. They call me the Child of France, but I don't know anything about it. I want to see the real France."

"The real France is starving and wretched. You don't want to see it."

"No. If things are as bad as that, Papa would do something about it. He loves the people of France," I insist.

"That doesn't feed anyone," Ernestine mumbles.

"If what you tell me is so, I want to see for myself," I say with conviction.

Ernestine shakes her curls at me. "You're mad!"

I lay my head on Ernestine's shoulder as I always do when trying to coax her into something. "Oh, please! You will help me do this, won't you? I am so bored here, and it would be such an adventure."

"Mad," she repeats. "But if you must go, you can get a ride from Jacques, who goes into Paris for supplies each week. If he thinks you're me, he won't object to giving you a ride there."

The guards open the gates of the courtyard so our horse-drawn cart can leave the palace. Sitting beside the rugged, earthy Jacques, a man of middle age, I suppress my intense excitement as the gates close behind us. It's really happening! I'm outside! On my own!

It's a full twelve miles from Versailles to Paris. In a plain dress borrowed from Ernestine, from a shabby cart, I will see so much of the countryside!

"So, Ernestine, how is the royal brat these days?" Jacques asks with a sort of snarl.

His words land like a slap. Why would he say such a thing? He doesn't even know me. "Don't call her that. She's nice," I manage to say.

"So you always insist," he scoffs. "Even though they have sent you to Paris on an errand like a common servant, you still defend them? I'm sure the princess is just as nice as that witch, her mother."

What? "Do you mean the queen?" I blurt too quickly to mask the indignation in my voice.

Jacques laughs coldly as he snaps his reins to drive the two horses forward into the town of Versailles.

"Yes, the Austrian spy," Jacques answers. His voice has dropped to a growl. "Madame Deficit who bankrupts the people to afford jewels and gowns and her lavish country house right on the grounds of the royal pig's palace."

My mouth opens to protest, but I am shocked beyond words. *The royal pig's palace? Madame Deficit? Austrian spy!*

I start to demand that he stop driving and let me off — but catch the words at the tip of my tongue. When will I have a chance like this again — a trip to and from Paris? So I sit silently, trying not to think of what I have heard.

Putting his words from my mind, I look all around, breathless with eagerness to see Paris at last.

CHAPTER 5

*P*aris *teems* with people! Men, women, and children over-
flow from the crowded doorways. They pour — laughing and
shouting, fighting and loving — from the windows. I'm knocked
and jostled as I climb from the cart into the street.

"Be here by eight tonight, or I'll leave without you," the horrible
Jacques informs me. I answer with a quick nod, averting my gaze. I
can't even stand to look at him.

In the next instant I am off, darting and weaving through the
crowd on the Place de la Concorde. I walk for hours and hours poking
my head into flower shops and dress shops, bakeries and bookstores.
In a wine store I am fascinated by the bottles of wavy blown glass
with their handwritten labels.

I see women with rouged faces loitering on corners. Rough-
looking men play cards in alleyways. I gaze at people who sit at the
outdoor cafés, and they look boldly back at me. No one curtsies or
bows — they don't even get out of my way to let me pass by — but
some smile and nod at me. A woman selling flowers gives me a
slightly wilted violet and waves me off with a gnarled hand when I
offer to pay with some coins Ernestine and I had collected.

I am fascinated and terrified, drawn in and holding back all in the same instant. No sight is too ugly. No smell too repugnant. I'm awhirl in a carousel of sensation!

I collide with a boy sweeping the street and am thrown down onto my rear. "Ow!"

"Hey, watch where you're going!" he cries indignantly.

"Sorry." I'm on the ground gazing up at him.

"What's the matter with you? Are you blind?" he continues to scold, extending a dirty hand to help me up. His hair is nearly black and curls around his ears and neck. It frames a lightly freckled face with bright green eyes flecked with amber.

"I'm sorry," I apologize again as he pulls me to standing. "I wasn't paying attention."

"Well, who goes around not paying attention?" he cries. "And you're still not — look!" I gaze down where he's pointing to discover that I am standing in a pile of dust and debris, my clogs covered in it. "I just swept all of that. Now I have to do it again."

"I said I was sorry, and it won't kill you to gather up this little bit of trash one more time," I reply irritably, unaccustomed to being so harshly scolded, especially for something that was unintentional.

The boy studies me with a neutral expression, and I gaze back at him. The vest he wears over a soiled white shirt is patched, and one scruffy boot has lifted from its worn sole, revealing only a bare foot. His face could be cleaner, and so could his abundant hair.

"Are you lost?" he asks.

"Why would you ask that?"

"I've never seen you before."

"Do you know everyone?" I challenge him doubtfully.

"In this neighborhood I do. Everyone comes into Dr. Curtius's exhibit eventually." He jerks his thumb over his shoulder at a sign that reads: DR. CURTIUS'S WAXWORKS EXHIBIT. "So, since I haven't seen you before, I know you're not from around here."

"Well, you're right. I'm not from around here."

"Then from where?"

"I work in the palace. I'm here on an errand and thought I'd have a look around Paris."

"You work at the palace!" the boy says in a fierce whisper. "Really?"

"Yes. Is that so remarkable?"

The boy's voice drops even lower and he leans in closer. "I wouldn't let people know you're from the palace."

"Why not? I'm only a maid."

"Even still . . . you never know."

"Know what?"

The boy checks to make sure no one is listening nearby. "If anyone asks, say you're from the countryside and you work on a farm."

"Why should I do that?" I'm starting to wonder if this fellow is in his right mind.

"Just listen to me and you'll be all right." His mood brightens. "Want to have a look inside?" he offers, his mouth turning up into a grin. "I can bring you in. I work here, cleaning up."

"I'd like to," I say. He beckons me to follow him in the front door. A woman dressed as a gypsy sits on a stool in a shadowy lobby and waves us through. She calls the boy Henri.

"Hello, Henri," I say when we are inside. "I'm Ernestine."

He shakes my hand, then gestures around the room where we stand.

"Take a look at this, Ernestine," Henri says. "It's something to see, isn't it?"

To my right, the great writer Voltaire sits at his desk, plume poised. Across the room, the tall and commanding Thomas Jefferson, the famous American revolutionary, laughs at something his colleague Benjamin Franklin is saying. In Paris, Franklin is as well regarded as Jefferson. I am told that they came to the palace when I was a child, but I can't remember them. "They're so real," I murmur admiringly.

Suddenly, I remember seeing the wax figure of Jefferson before. Mademoiselle Grosholtz!

"Does Mademoiselle Grosholtz make these figures?" I ask.

Henri stares at me, puzzled. "How do you —?" Then his face clears and he nods. "She teaches at the palace! Of course!"

"Yes, I've seen her there. She was working on this Jefferson one day when I went into the art room."

"Dr. Curtius taught her how to copy people like this," Henri tells me. "But I think she's becoming even better at it than he is." Henri seems to remember something and laughs. "She *did* make the great Citizen Jefferson at the palace," he confirms with a smile. "You should have seen the excitement it caused on the day she stepped out of her coach lugging the wax figure. Our customers were sure that Jefferson was back in town. Everyone in Paris came to see him."

"Were they disappointed to discover that it was only a wax figure?" I ask.

"I thought they would be, but they weren't," Henri says thoughtfully. "The figure was so realistic that they felt as though they'd really seen him. At least no one complained or asked for their money back."

"He *is* very lifelike," I say. "Why did you call him *Citizen* Jefferson?"

"Do you hear nothing in the palace?" Henri asks, looking serious.

I don't know how to answer. I'm not sure what he means.

"These days in Paris, everyone is called Citizen. The revolutionaries want to do away with titles. No more Monsieur or Madame. It's all Citizen this and Citizen that. We are all equal, you see."

I blink. Several times. This is an idea my mind can't quite take in. "No more Your Highness?" I ask.

Henri tosses his head back, laughing. "Especially not that! If the revolutionaries have their way, all the royalty will be cut down to size. They will be citizens, too. Of course there are those who disagree, but if you ask me, that's the way the wind is blowing."

"Oh my," I say. I had no idea such a thing was even possible.

"Come look at this." Henri yanks aside a purple velvet curtain, and I gasp.

This part of the exhibit is called *Ancient Rome*. Toga-clad figures stand among white pillars. "Is he supposed to be Julius Caesar?" I ask, pointing at a man in a purple toga who wears a crown of olive leaves.

"That's him," Henri says. He pulls me over to a fat figure playing a violin. "This is Emperor Nero. People say the royal family is like him. He fiddled around with his violin while all of Rome burned."

"Paris isn't burning," I object, trying not to sound as indignant as I feel.

"It's burning, all right," Henri insists. "Burning with talk of overthrowing the aristocracy."

"That will never happen," I state firmly. My mind is starting to clear. Just because Henri thinks revolution is brewing doesn't mean it's so. He's hardly an educated person. "The people love the royal family; they've loved them for hundreds of years," I add.

Henri shrugs. "If you say so. Since you love the royals so much, you might like to see this." He leads me into another room, and all at once I'm back at Versailles.

"It's me!" I cry.

Henri's head snaps around toward me, startled. "What did you say?"

"Ah, me!" I lie to cover my gaff. I'm agape at the tableaux of wax figures before me. Imitations of my family sit at a long luxurious table heaped with all sorts of delicious food. Their clothing is opulent, as are the furniture, carpets, and drapery. It's a familiar scene. Mama wears one of her white muslin gowns. My brother, Louis-Charles, feeds one of the palace dogs under the table. The figure that resembles me with an uncanny likeness has a book smuggled onto her lap just the way I often have.

Tears creep into my eyes when I notice the empty cradle in the corner. It's for my infant sister, Sophie, who died at only eleven months old. Such a dear, sweet baby! There is also an empty chair at the table, and I guess it's to represent Louis-Joseph, the older of my two younger brothers, who died of a lung disease. How I still miss him!

"Why are you suddenly so sad?" Henri asks. His eyes reveal deep concern.

"The empty cradle," I say, pressing my hands to my eyes to dry them. "The baby and her brother were so dear. Their family misses them with all their hearts."

"Hearts?" Henri questions skeptically. "Do any of them actually possess a heart?"

"Of course they do!" I snap at him.

"You'd never know it, not from the way they treat their subjects," Henri says with a disdain that is casual yet clearly heartfelt. "They don't care about anyone but themselves."

"That's not true."

Henri takes hold of my hand and looks into my eyes. "Ernestine, I can tell *you've* got a kind, good heart. You think the best of everyone, even the selfish royals. I'm glad you bashed into me today."

"You are?" I ask.

"We'll be the best of friends, always."

"I hope so, Henri," I say.

CHAPTER 6

Now that I have met Henri, the palace can't contain me. I long to be out in Paris, walking with him, laughing at the odd street characters we pass, sharing a crêpe made outdoors on flat metal stoves.

One day, I am strolling with Henri, and he nods toward a grate in the street. "Ever been down there?"

"Down in a sewer?" I ask, puzzled. "Of course not. Why would I go down there?"

Henri laughs. "I've *lived* down there."

"Really?" Is he joking?

He nods. "When we first arrived in Paris, after we left our farm, my brothers and I were homeless. Sometimes whole families live down there. It's not that unusual."

"Paris seems full of apartments and houses. Why would you choose a sewer?"

Again Henri laughs grimly. "Haven't you ever heard of landlords?" When I shake my head, he continues, "Landlords own apartments and houses. They expect to be paid for the use of their property."

"Are there really people so poor that they can't pay the landlords?"

"Yes. Many of them are that poor." Henri faces me. "You've been living at the palace much too long. Do you live as lavishly as the clueless royals?"

"Not at first. My family lived in the servants' quarters when I was younger, but I'm an orphan now and they let me be educated with the princess and share in many of her privileges."

"Then you're very lucky, I'd say. No wonder you don't think badly of the royal family. Why would you ever want to leave the palace?"

"Why did your family decide to leave the farm?"

"They didn't decide. The king's men conscripted my father and older brothers to work on a new roadway."

"Conscripted?" I asked.

"It means forced. They had to leave the farm, and right at harvest — for no pay."

"Couldn't they explain that they had to farm their land?"

"You *have* been sheltered, haven't you?" Henri says with a laugh. "You don't say no to the king's soldiers — not if you want to live. With my father and oldest brothers away, we lost that season's crop and were left with nothing. My mother sent some of us older ones into the city to fend for ourselves. I live with my two brothers, though I don't see much of them."

"That's terrible," I say. "I'm sure the king has no idea this sort of thing is going on."

My statement makes Henri rock with laughter. "I've never met anyone so unaware of the real world."

"I know plenty!" I object. "Can you read?"

"Of course not."

"I can!"

Henri's face softens. "I'm sorry, Ernestine. I don't mean to insult you. It's not your fault that you work at the palace. I'm just saying that there's another world outside the palace and it's as different as it could ever be."

My indignation is softened by the tenderness in his tone. "That's why I'm here," I explain more calmly, "to see the real Paris that I'm missing."

The rain has slowed to a drizzle when we arrive in front of a palace with many columns in front. Though not nearly as grand as Versailles, it is still impressive, taking up blocks and blocks and facing an expansive cobblestoned plaza. "This is the palace of the duc d'Orléans and his wife," Henri explains.

I recognize the name. He is a nobleman, a royal relative, whom my mother despises, saying he is treacherous and cowardly. Despite his royal title, his family has no real wealth. Henri tells me that to make extra money the duc has built a wooden platform at the edge of his palace grounds and rents out pavilions and arcades for popular entertainment. "How low class," I say.

"I suppose so," Henri says with a shrug. "But it's fun."

Henri takes my hand, and we race across the plaza. As we go, the crowd gets increasingly thick. The air is filled with the cries of merchants selling their wares. Red, white, and blue ladies' hand fans seem to be all the rage and are on sale everywhere. I try on a three-sided hat but it's too big. Henri and I share a sausage cooked on an outdoor grill and wrapped into a fresh roll. I nearly faint from its deliciousness.

Here there is every kind of fascinating act: sword-swallowers, exotic dancers in satin gowns, poodles that walk a tight wire, a man who is four hundred pounds, a woman who is seven feet tall.

I love the smell of food, the press of people. Henri and I come upon a man playing a violin.

"Can you dance?" I ask Henri.

He breaks into a jig. I recognize it as the same movements the maid taught me. I join him, laughing. A small crowd forms around us, clapping along and singing. They applaud when the song ends.

Henri and I bow together, shoulder to shoulder, both of us smiling. "You're wonderful, Ernestine!" Henri praises my dancing.

"You too," I return the compliment.

He takes hold of my hand, and I curl my fingers into his as we wander together back into the crowd.

Henri takes me in to see the exhibit called *The Belle Zulima*, a woman who still looks beautiful, even though her corpse is supposedly over two hundred years old. Placed in a glass coffin, she is dressed in an outfit from the Orient that is no more than a short, sea-green top that reveals her belly and matching flowing pants.

The crowd viewing *The Belle Zulima*, mostly men, circle, admiring her. I stand at her head, fixated by her lovely face, so serene and free of any blemish or wrinkle. I wonder if she is truly a corpse or made of wax. My concentration is so great that my nose touches the glass case as I try to see in the shadowy light of the tent.

All at once her blue eyes open. And she winks!

My heart leaps and I scream, jumping away from the case.

Everyone stares at me. Too startled to speak, I point at Belle Zulima.

But her eyes are closed once more and she lies in the case serenely supine.

Didn't anyone else see her move? Apparently not.

Flustered and embarrassed by the gaze of the crowd, I run out of the tent and spy Henri among the people watching a man who is standing on a wooden crate orating. Breathless with fear, I clutch his arm. "You won't believe what happened!"

"Belle Zulima winked at you?"

"How did you know?"

"She does that every now and then. They say it's good luck if Belle Zulima winks at you."

"You mean she's alive?" I ask.

Henri laughs. "Of course she is. It's only a show."

"Then why do the men pay to see her if they know she's not really a two-hundred-year-old corpse?"

"She's pretty."

"How does she stay still for so long?" I wonder.

"I don't know," Henri says. "She models for the wax museum sometimes; the figure of Venus looks just like her."

"Death to tyrants!" the orator cries, startling me. "May their blood flow in the streets of Paris. Let no citizen flinch from the duty of seizing freedom!" The speaker has a squat, gnarled body and hunched shoulders. His blistered skin is flushed red with zeal.

"Who is that?" I ask Henri.

"Jean-Paul Marat. He publishes a paper."

"What kind of paper?"

"I don't know. I can't read it." He walks to a table that is stacked with folded papers and hands me one.

I read a headline that cries out for the deaths of the royal family, and my hands begin to tremble. They accuse my parents of having bankrupted the people. A hideous cartoon shows my mother sitting on the lap of some nobleman. My father is depicted as a large pig wearing a crown.

So much hatred directed at my family!

Henri snaps the paper from me. "I'm sorry, Ernestine. I just saw the cartoons. You shouldn't be reading this." He notices my shaking and cradles my hands in his own.

In the warmth of his clasp, I stop quaking with fear. "The people he wants to kill are my friends. Would they murder the servants as well as the aristocrats?"

"Don't be afraid, Ernestine. I won't let anything happen to you."

"You can't protect me," I protest.

"I can. You'll see. A new world is coming — can you feel it?"

I shake my head.

"When the new world comes, every person will be equal and all of us will be free from tyranny. Life will be better for all of us."

"Do you really believe that?" I ask.

Studying my face, he nods. "My brothers are involved in the fight, right at the center of things. They say a new day is dawning for France. But don't you worry. You can count on me, Ernestine. I promise."

CHAPTER 7

The more I get to know Paris, the clearer is my idea of what Henri has been telling me. Filthy children live on the street, working hard for the little they have to eat. Sick and ragged mothers beg with outstretched hands while rocking naked infants. Dogs with protruding ribs roam the streets.

I notice other groups of women who gather in the doorways of stores, speaking in hushed tones. Their hands are always busy with knitting or crochet work, and they watch all who go by with suspicious, narrowed glares. I can feel their eyes on me as we pass them. "What are they doing?" I ask Henri.

"It's not only the men who are angry about the way things are," he tells me. "The women talk, too, and sometimes they're even more thirsty for blood than the men. Many of them have watched their children die of starvation."

I remember the rage in the women's faces the night they marauded through Versailles. I was young when that happened but old enough to be terrified. The women broke into the palace and stormed up the stairs, demanding food. They got as far as Mama's bedroom and sliced up the sheets. Luckily, Mama, Louis-Charles, and I escaped to Papa's quarters through a secret passage.

"What do the women talk about?" I ask.

He leans closer to me. "Revolution," he whispers.

Revolution?! The word makes my throat tighten as if someone is clutching it in a viselike grip.

With animal instinct, I feel the women's eyes boring into the back of my head and swing around to check. As I suspected, their gazes are still locked on me.

Snapping back around, I clutch Henri's arm to steady myself, for I feel dizzy with fear. "Why are they staring?" I hiss in a panic. Henri shrugs casually, but I pray it's not recognition as we hurry on.

On our way to the Palais-Royal, we stroll past a man selling red-white-and-blue-striped ribbons fanned into a kind of layered circle like the one Henri wears on his jacket. I know that it's a sign of support for the revolutionaries. Henri buys one of them from the man and pins it to the side of my shirt. "You'd better wear the tricolor, too," he advises.

"No!" I insist, taking it off. "I don't want to wear it."

"It's safer, trust me."

"I don't care!" I'm not wearing the hateful thing, and he can't make me.

Henri drags me off the street into an alley. He clutches my arm too tightly. I don't like it and shake him off harshly.

I'm still holding the ribbon, and I toss it into a puddle. "Don't ever try to put this on me again!" I shout.

Lunging at me, Henri covers my mouth with his hand. "Be quiet," he hisses in my ear.

I pry his hand away. Unexpectedly, my eyes brim with tears, and this show of weakness mortifies me. Breaking away from him, I turn to face into the alley. "Go away," I say. "Leave me alone."

Standing there trembling with emotion, I wait until I hear his retreating footsteps. Only then do I pull in a deep breath and try to steady myself.

This is all such torment. I understand how it all seems to Henri. I see the squalor, the poverty, the unfairness of it all. I'm not blind!

But to join his cause?! We're talking about my family! These people hate us with a burning fire. They talk about *killing* Mama and Papa along with many of our dearest friends. How can I be in favor of *that*?

But how can I blame Henri? He doesn't know who I really am. I long to tell him, but it would put him in an impossible position. And perhaps it's myself I'm thinking of. I don't believe he'd ever reveal my secret, but what if he shunned me?

I couldn't bear that.

Looking to the puddle, I see that the tricolor ribbon is gone. Henri must have picked it up.

He only wants to protect me.

I walk out of the alley and Henri is waiting, leaning up against the building. "Sorry to be so rough, Ernestine," he says. "Do you understand that I don't want anything to happen to you?"

I nod. "But you must understand that the people they talk about harming are my friends."

"Ernestine, I've never wanted to mention this . . . I didn't want to upset you," Henri says quietly. "But you know, don't you, how much you resemble the princess?"

My jaw drops. I didn't realize he'd noticed. But, of course, he is familiar with the wax likeness. "I suppose I do."

"You suppose?"

"All right! I do look like her. I know it," I say, throwing my arms wide in pretend exasperation. "It's just a coincidence."

Henri leans in close. "Learn to whisper," he advises softly. Henri slips the ribbon into the pocket of my skirt. "If you won't wear it, keep it nearby. Your life may depend on it someday."

"Do you know where Mademoiselle Grosholtz has been?" I ask him as we walk back toward the exhibit.

"She still goes to the palace but she is spending more and more time helping Dr. Curtius."

"What new figures is she doing?"

"She's done a figure of Madame de Pompadour and Madame du Barry in an exhibit called *Royal Consorts*."

"But how did she model them? Madame de Pompadour is dead and Madame du Barry has gone to England."

"She often uses portraits and death masks."

"Death masks?" I cry, alarmed by the sound of it. "What's that?"

"It's an ancient tradition, taking a cast of a dead person's face right after the person dies," he explains. "Mademoiselle Grosholtz told me that the ancient Egyptians made them. She showed me some death masks Dr. Curtius has in his collection. Some are coated with gold or silver or bronze. They're creepy."

"What other figures has she done?" I ask.

"The king's cousin, the duc d'Orléans, was posing the other day. Mademoiselle Grosholtz was talking to him." I make a face, not being overfond of my self-impressed uncle. This causes Henri to laugh. "I suppose you know them all, don't you?"

"I guess I do," I admit. "They're just people. No different from me or you."

Henri laughs so hard that he staggers backward. "Ernestine, sometimes I just can't believe the things you say."

CHAPTER 8

One night I return and Ernestine is waiting for me just inside the kitchen door, dressed in my finest gown. "What took you so long?" she scolds in a whisper.

The kitchen staff and servants bow and curtsy as we pass. Everyone knows that Ernestine and Madame Royale have a special friendship, so no one is surprised to see us together — only they think she is me and I am she. Ernestine speaks so quickly I can't understand what she's saying. "Take a breath to calm yourself," I advise her.

"Your cousin the duc d'Angoulême is here," she tells me more slowly. "I have been entertaining him for *hours* pretending to be you."

I have only seen my cousin twice before, when we were much younger. I remember him as a nice boy, quiet and polite. He is seventeen or eighteen years of age by now.

"Is Louis-Antoine nice?" I ask hopefully.

"Wonderful!" she replies with a sigh. A sigh? Is she smitten with Louis-Antoine?

But there is no time to ask.

"Thank goodness he's a decent fellow," I tell her as we hurry on through the halls, "because he is my intended." I suddenly wonder if I've ever told her that before.

I needn't wonder for long because her expression is completely dumbstruck. "Marry Louis-Antoine?!" she exclaims. "Oh, you are the luckiest girl in the world!"

A smile spreads across my face at this. I have spent a lot of time imagining how the round-faced, cherubic little boy would grow. As a child he had a striking resemblance to my father, who — though I adore him completely — is not the handsomest man in the world. "Can you tell he's a Bourbon?" I ask, since all the Bourbon family on my father's side have the same unfortunate appearance.

"His mother must be very beautiful," she answers with tact. "Just as you favor your lovely mother in looks, so must Louis-Antoine resemble his, for he is quite handsome."

I clasp her hands. "Good! Very good!" It's no doubt shallow of me, but I would hate to be betrothed to an ugly man.

In my bedroom, we change clothing in a flurry of thrown petticoats, stockings, and dresses. "He must wonder what's become of you. I've been gone so long," Ernestine worries.

My hair is disheveled but there is no time to fix it. I will have to think of some excuse. "Hurry!" she urges me and nearly pushes me out into the sitting room where my cousin awaits.

"You're back!" he cries happily, standing. "I thought maybe you'd forgotten about me."

"I'm sorry, cousin," I say.

"You forgot. I asked you to call me Antoine."

"Sorry, Antoine."

"You've changed your hairstyle?" He notices.

"Ah, yes. That's what took me so long. The wig I was wearing was hot and I needed to take it off."

"So this is now your own hair, then?"

"Yes."

"It's very lovely."

"Thank you."

I sit, and then he sits. Ernestine was right that he's grown to be a handsome young man. His blond hair is wavy and short. You can tell he's a Bourbon, but other familial influences have improved on the unfortunate Bourbon features.

"So, what brings you here?" I ask to break the awkward silence that has fallen between us.

"You have a short memory. Weren't we just talking about it a brief while ago?"

I answer with a forced giggle. "How foolish of me! Of course we were. Well, I am very glad you were able to fit me into your schedule."

He seems confused. "As I said, Father has business to discuss with the king, and I asked him to bring me so I could see you."

"Of course. You did say that, didn't you?"

I am afraid to say anything more for fear of further revealing that I have no idea of what he and Ernestine have been talking about these several hours. More uncomfortable silence follows.

Antoine coughs.

"Some water?" I offer.

"No. Thank you."

I smile tensely. "How is your mother?"

"Fine." He taps the table and then smiles a bit stiffly. "I fear I've worn you out."

"How so?"

"You were so lively until you went off to change your wig. We were getting on so well. Now you seem changed in some way."

I'm tempted to just tell him the truth, but I don't dare. It's been so long since I've seen him, I don't know if I can trust him with my secret. Obviously, Ernestine and he have warmed to each other, but to me, he's like a stranger.

He stands and takes my hand. "It's funny to think that we shall be married before too long. You've become such a beauty."

I like the compliment, but oddly, something about it rankles me. "Is that what you wanted to find out?" I ask.

He blushes again and nods.

I have to smile at his shyness — and his honesty. I can't really blame him for wishing to assess me, since I wanted to know the same thing about him. "Do you think we'll be happy together?" I ask.

At this his expression becomes thoughtful. "It's hard to say. If you're really like the person you were just before, then yes. If you are more often as you are now . . ." He hesitates. "I'm sure it is just that I have fatigued you."

It's true that I'm tired. I have been walking for hours through Paris.

"Can I ask you something?" I say suddenly, thinking of the day I've just spent. "Do you think the people of France hate us?"

Some emotion behind his eyes flares. Surprise at my boldness? Fear? "I think they do," he says with feeling.

"Why?"

"I hear talk. In fact, my father is here to speak with your father about that very fact. Papa believes a revolution could be brewing."

Revolution! He fears it, too. It's not just me who is so upset by the talk. His words let me know that this threat is real, and a chill runs through me.

"My father thinks we Bourbons should flee the country," Antoine adds.

"Flee!" I cry, shocked.

"Yes, while it's still possible."

An image of Henri's face flashes into my mind. "No! We can't leave France. It's impossible."

Never to see Henri again? Unthinkable!

"Your father is wrong," I insist passionately. "We are the royal family. This is our country, and we must address the problem before the people are pushed too far. There's still time. I know it! We can never leave. Never!"

CHAPTER 9

*H*enri and I meet at the Place de la Concorde and I immediately notice something new on the plaza — a very tall rectangular object. Even in the dusty city, a blade gleams from halfway up the frame from which it's suspended. "What's that?" I ask.

Henri looks at me and his face is deadly serious. "It's called a guillotine."

"What does it do?"

Henri takes a deep breath before answering. "It cuts off heads."

His words make me recoil with horror. "Why do they need a killing mechanism?"

"They say it's merciful," Henri says bitterly, "swifter and faster than the executioner's axe."

This is horrible. "How many heads do they intend to sever?" I ask as the realization of this new invention sinks into my mind. "Who are the people they intend to kill?"

Henri covers his face with his hand as a shudder runs through him.

"What is it? What's the matter?" I urge him to tell me.

"They have taken her, Ernestine! Last night they came for Mademoiselle Grosholtz!"

I look sharply at the guillotine. Is he telling me that Mademoiselle Grosholtz is to be one of its victims? It can't be! "Who has taken her?" I ask Henri. "Taken her where?"

"The people have formed their own army. They're arresting anyone thought to be an aristocrat or a friend of the royal family. Everyone knows Mademoiselle Grosholtz works at the palace. They say she's spying on revolutionaries and reporting their activities to the king."

"That's not true. I never saw her talking to my . . . to the king."

"She talks to the king's sister, though," Henri says. "I once asked her what she thought of the Revolution, and she said she didn't care about it. She just wanted to be left alone to make her wax figures."

"Can't she tell them that? They'll let her go if she does, won't they?"

Henri shakes his head. "It's not enough to say you don't care. You have to be *for* the Revolution."

Suddenly, I jolt to my feet. An open cart rumbles by, and in the back stand two women with their hands bound. Henri is immediately by my side, mouth ajar. We exchange horrified glances.

One woman is tall and beautiful with large, dark eyes and tight black curls. Beside her is Mademoiselle Grosholtz!

A million emotions play across Henri's anguished face.

I grip Henri's arm.

People in the street are eyeing Mademoiselle and the other woman darkly, but no one speaks. A man spits in the gutter.

"Mademoiselle!" I cry.

She turns toward me. Her eyes widen in alarm. She sees Henri and seems even more stricken. Then she averts her gaze, deliberately ignoring us, gazing up into the gray sky.

Behind me a window is shattered, and so is the silence. Angry cries and hissing voices fill the air, and the hair on the back of my neck prickles as a chill breeze blows across the square. "The king has dismissed Necker!" someone shouts.

I know that name. Jacques Necker is the minister of finance. He speaks on behalf of the people and is popular with them.

The people who had been milling about in the street pick up the cry, "Necker is dismissed!" They start to run toward us and hurl things into the air. I flinch as more glass is broken.

"Death to tyrants!" a woman shouts. A guard steps into the street. His knees buckle when someone hurls a rock at his head.

Some are blood-smeared, their clothing torn. I see that most wear the red-white-and-blue ribbons, the tricolor.

A group of shouting people break down the front door of a patisserie. The terrified baker is passed over the heads of the crowd, struggling and screaming. He is sucked down into the horde and they begin kicking him.

It's too hideous!

I turn away and see the cart carrying Mademoiselle Grosholtz and the other woman disappear around a corner. I'm glad it's moving away from the contraption with the menacing blade. The sight of the looming guillotine sickens me.

Black clouds blow into view, tumbling over one another with ominous movement. "Let's go inside," Henri suggests, taking hold of my elbow. "It's about to storm."

Henri leads me up a dark staircase into a very small apartment. "Georges? Pierre?" he calls, but no one replies. "My brothers must be out," he says, lighting a candle.

In the gray light, I see three straw-stuffed mattresses thrown on the floor. Dirty dishes are piled in a rusted sink. Three rough-hewn chairs and an oil lamp are the only other furnishings.

Henri laughs at the shocked expression on my face. "It's not exactly the palace, I know." He heads to the window and looks down at the street. "But at least we're safe from that."

Distant thunder rumbles. Or so I think. I move to Henri's side to see the rioting just beneath the window and realize I've been hearing the roar of the crowd amassed below.

Henri gasps as someone smashes the front window of Dr. Curtius's waxworks across the street. In the next moment, the door of the exhibit is thrown open and people run inside the exhibition.

"Why did they do that?" I ask, distressed.

Before Henri can answer, my hand flies over my mouth to stifle a scream. Carried out of the exhibit, each on its own spike, are the heads of Papa and Mama, looking extraordinarily lifelike.

"You're sure they're wax?" I ask Henri desperately. "They couldn't be real?"

"Yes! Of course they're wax. They're from the exhibit I showed you. I see them every day." He pushes me gently from the window. "Don't look."

Suddenly, the sky opens and a torrent of rain teems down. I watch, hoping the people will scramble for cover, but they don't even seem to notice the rain.

My heart pounds. "I have to get home," I say, going toward the door.

Henri grabs my arm. "You can't go out in that. You'll be trampled."

"I have to get back to them at the palace," I insist.

"What do the royals need you for? To sweep the floor? To play cards with the princess?"

"You don't understand! My friends are there." That much at least is true.

"They're in a palace, Ernestine. They have gates and soldiers all around them. Besides, they're twelve miles away from here."

But I can't help reenvisioning the sights and sounds I've just witnessed. The windows of stores being smashed in. The homes of wealthy citizens being broken into and all their possessions tossed into the street where the mob grabs at the flying objects. And they've gotten to Versailles before! Closing my eyes, I once again relive the night when I was a girl and we scrambled through secret passageways to escape their murderous rampage.

Returning to the window, I can't help but look down as my parents' heads are carried on spikes while the people spit, jeer, and throw rocks. The mob has armed itself with guns, pikes, and iron hooks. I watch as they drag another baker from his shop and someone throws a rope noose around his neck. As they drag him down the street, I turn away, trying not to imagine what the crowd intends to do with him, though knowing just the same.

"I have to go home," I repeat in a trembling whisper.

"All right. All right," Henri agrees. "Wait a few minutes until the crowd moves on. Then we'll go the back ways to the Place de la Concorde and meet your driver."

"I hate to see that horrible thing again," I say, thinking of the mechanism with the blade. "Tell me again what it's called."

"The guillotine. A doctor with that name invented it, I hear."

"Oh, that's right. The merciful Dr. Guillotin," I recall, my voice dripping with bitter irony. "It's hard to believe that the hideous contraption contains an ounce of mercy in it."

I tremble, unable to stop, remembering the heads on the spikes. Tears run down my cheeks. If they would behead Mademoiselle Grosholtz just for giving art lessons at the palace, how many others would they murder? Everyone at Versailles?

My terror becomes so awful I can't stand it. "I have to go!" I insist, heading for the door. Henri is right behind me as I fling it open and hurry back down the stairs.

I run into the street and mingle with the enraged, roaring crowd. They're shouting and demanding bread and flour. They call for death to the royal traitors.

CHAPTER 10

As soon as I hit the street, with Henri right behind me, I know that the crowd, with its weapons and tricolors and murderous rage, is heading for Versailles.

After being pushed and nearly knocked down, I despair of making it all the way to the Place de la Concorde to meet Jacques, and so it seems like a happy dream when I see him, his cart rocked to and fro as he makes his way through the mob.

"Jacques!" I cry, flailing my arms for his attention.

"Ernestine!" he shouts, returning my waves.

Turning, I touch Henri's cheek with a quick kiss. He clasps my wrist. "You're crazy to go back there," he says.

For a second, I hesitate, but I need to be with my family. "I have to," I say, as I break free of his grasp. "I'll see you soon!"

It isn't easy to make my way through the crowd to Jacques, but once I do he pulls me up onto the front seat beside him. "They won't get inside the gates," Jacques says confidently. "But we must get there before the mob does."

We ride back to Versailles through the rainstorm at breakneck speed and arrive ahead of the mob. I'm soaked and spattered with mud, but so relieved to see the palace. "We have to warn everyone," I say to Jacques as I climb down.

"Just stay away from the royal quarters," he advises. "The royal family are the ones the crowd wants. They will get everything they deserve now."

I ignore him and race into the palace, running straight for my bedroom. "Ernestine, how did you get so wet and dirty?" asks Madame Campan, Mama's waiting lady, who has just come out of my room.

"I was in the courtyard in the rain," I say as I pull off my dress and yank another frock over my head. Quickly brushing out my wet locks, I pile them atop my head with a cord.

"Have you seen the princess?" Madame Campan asks.

"No," I say curtly as I run past her, down the hall toward Papa's chambers.

I burst into Papa's meeting room despite knowing that he's in conference with his advisers and ministers. "You have to close the gates!" I cry out. "The people are coming from Paris. They're demanding bread."

Everyone stares at me in alarm.

"How do you know this?" Papa asks.

"Ernestine tells me that — the servants are hearing things," I say, a sort of half-truth.

"Perhaps the gates should be locked, as a precaution," one of the advisers suggests.

Papa considers this for several moments and then rises from his chair. "If the people need bread, then we will open the royal storehouses to them," he says.

"What if there's not enough bread for all of them?" another adviser asks.

"Then we'll give them flour to make their own," Papa replies.

I know he's not understanding the truth of what's coming. How can I make him see the frenzy and fury of the people heading this way? "Have someone bring the bread outside the farthest gate," I say. "That way they won't come any closer."

Papa smiles at me. "What a smart girl you are," he says with a nod. "Now go to Mama and tell her what is happening. She and her ladies should take refuge in the royal apartments. You and your brother must accompany her there."

"And Ernestine, too?"

"Yes, of course. Ernestine, too."

Papa turns to his advisers. "Perhaps the queen and the children should be moved to the palace at Fontainebleau. Or perhaps to Rambouillet. Which would be easiest to escape to?"

"I'll consult the captain of the guard for his opinion," one of the ministers says, and exits the room.

"Will you be leaving, as well, Your Highness?" someone asks.

Papa shakes his head. "No. I must stay and help my people through this."

I am not sure whether I feel pride at my papa's quiet conviction or frightened at what his subjects may do to him. To us all. Slipping through the door behind a minister, I run back to the royal apartments. I find Ernestine first.

"Why did you ever come back?" she asks. "You were safer outside the palace."

"I had to warn everyone," I say. "And I couldn't be away at a time such as this."

Ernestine hugs me. "You're more than a sister to me," she says with a sob in her voice. "You're a sister and a very best friend at once."

"We are one," I say. "That's why we look alike. We're one soul with two bodies."

There are tears in Ernestine's eyes as she nods in agreement and takes my hand. "Nothing can ever separate us."

"Come. Let's go find the queen and tell her what's happening."

When Ernestine and I find Mama, she's in her chambers with Louis-Charles and her ladies. In a fast torrent of words, I tell her everything that's happened.

"Should I pack, Your Highness?" one of her ladies asks.

"Pack some things just in case, but I don't expect to leave. Our place is here with the king," Mama replies. I walk with her to the window and gaze across the glistening courtyards. The rain has subsided and the wet stones seem to glow pink in the sunset. In the distance beyond the palace gates, the raucous crowd approaches like a wave toward the shore.

"The gates will keep them out," Mama assures us. Just the same, my hand trembles.

While Mama helps her ladies pack, Ernestine and I step outside and wander the halls. We hear murmurs throughout the palace. They say that in the forefront of the mob are tough rugged women from the fish markets, still in their blood-smeared aprons, their fish-gutting knives at the ready.

Ernestine and I stare at each other in shocked horror as the next news sweeps through the servants' quarters. The mob has broken through the gates. The fish market women have beaten and sliced at the sentinel guards, overpowering them. At the same time, another group has found an unprotected gate and slipped inside the palace grounds.

"It will be all right," Ernestine says as we hurry back to Mama's apartments. "The Swiss guard will protect us."

"Papa is giving them bread," I agree. "That's what they really want."

But we get the bad news delivered to Mama by a maid. When Papa offered delegates from the crowd carts of bread and flour from the two palace granaries, it's not enough. The mob is past wanting bread. Now they are after blood.

I'm terrified for her safety when Mama parts the windows and steps out onto her terrace to face the crowd.

They are amazed, and for a moment the people stare in stunned silence.

I, too, hold my breath, awed by her bravery.

She bows to them, a long, low curtsy.

"We'll roast the queen's heart tomorrow!" someone shouts. This is all the mob needs to be set off, and their outraged shouts become a roar.

Mama backs away, returning inside. I lunge for the window, latching it.

All of us — Mama, her ladies, Ernestine, Louis-Charles, and I — sleep fitfully in the apartments together that night while the crowd outside grows larger and larger. From the window I see the duc d'Orléans strutting at the front of the crowd. Mama was right, it seems, not to trust him.

In the middle of the night, I jolt upright, awakened by a clamor. We learn that the people have broken into the palace. Guards scuttle us from one room to the next to keep us safe. Despite their care, I see things: walls smeared with blood, ripped bedding, smashed windows, a crystal chandelier shattered on the floor. I hear screams and shouting, crying and gunshots.

Ernestine and I run behind my parents down a spiraling hidden passage I've never seen before. At the end of the passage, outside the door, six carriages wait to take us to safety.

The carriages are soon spotted by the crowd, which gathers around to impede our progress. Severed heads of some of the guards are put on pikes and carried alongside our carriage. I refuse to look, though Ernestine gapes through the coach windows, fixated with horror at the sight. Louis-Charles hugs Mama, who sits calm and serious. The window crashes and something wrapped in cloth lands on the lap of Madame de Tourzel, who has replaced Madame Polignac as our governess. Father snaps it up and hurls it back out the window.

Slowly, slowly we travel onward.

"The people have demanded my return to Paris," Papa explains. "I must do whatever it takes to calm them."

Mama takes his hand and squeezes it.

The carriage turns off the road near an inn for a bathroom break. For the moment, we've outrun the crowd. "Everyone be quick," Papa tells us.

When I go to follow the others inside, Papa takes hold of my wrist and stops me. Mama is beside him.

I look at them, puzzled. "What is it?"

Mama's eyes brim with tears.

"We're going to leave you here, Marie-Thérèse," Papa says.

"What?" I cry.

"My brother, your uncle, whom you've met at the palace, is coming from Austria to get you," Mama says. "I got a message out to him before we left. He has promised me that if such a thing as this were to happen, he would come here for you."

"Why me?" I ask. "Why not all of us?"

"He can smuggle you out, and Ernestine will stand in for you. No one will notice. If we all try to get out, they'll surely stop us at the border. And besides, your father refuses to leave his people, and my place is beside him."

Gazing around, I see no uncle there to take me off. "Where is he?" I ask.

Papa opens a bag and produces a large handful of money. He presses it into my hand. "Stay here. Sleep on the ground, if you must, but wait for him."

Mama takes a bundle of clothing from under the seat. "Change into these simple clothes." She pulls the ribbon and pins from my hair, messing it. "Say you work at one of these farms if anyone asks. Stay out of sight altogether, if you can."

I don't want to do this, to be separated from my family. "When will I see you all again?" I ask, a desperate sob rising in my voice.

Mama holds my arms. "You must be brave, Marie-Thérèse," she says. "You're not a child anymore. You are my Mousseline Serieuse — delicate but strong. You can do this."

"But why must I?" I ask.

"You'll be safe in Austria. My family has promised to come with an army to help us. When that happens, you will be a legitimate member of the Bourbon family who can take her place on the throne once more. You'll have supporters who will rally to your side."

"What about you and Papa? Won't they rally to your side?"

Papa and Mama exchange a quick look, and I don't like it. What do they fear will happen to them?

"We hope so," Papa says. "Until the time of our rescue, though, we want one member of the family to remain free."

The others are returning from the inn. How can I leave Mama and Papa? Louis-Charles and Ernestine?

Ernestine comes beside me. "Did you know about this?" I ask her. She nods.

"It's not fair that you should take my place," I say.

"It's all right," she answers. "Your uncle will come and his army will restore order. We'll see each other again soon."

"No!" I cry, hugging her to me.

Papa pries us apart and ushers Ernestine into the coach. "Go behind those bushes, change into these clothes, and wait for your uncle," he commands. "No tears, now. Ernestine is correct. We'll see one another soon."

Before I even reach the nearest bush, the coach is rattling away from me. Ernestine stretches out the window to wave to me, her face drenched in tears.

As soon as I see her tearful expression, tears explode from my eyes as well. I can't believe this is happening. It's so unreal.

Ernestine disappears from the window, and I watch the coach until it's out of sight. Then I change into the plain gray dress and worn boots. I tie the white apron around my waist and pull on the white mobcap. I stuff my own gown into the bushes.

Then I sit and wait for my uncle to come from Austria. For three days I live on apples from a nearby orchard, but no uncle arrives.

Deciding that I can't stay there forever, I begin to walk. A woman driving a cart full of lambs slows to offer me a ride. "I'm headed for Paris," she says. "Where are you going?"

"Paris," I answer. "I'm headed to Paris, too."

PART II
THE TERROR

CHAPTER 11

*I*n the year that I've been in Paris, I think I have changed completely. At first I stayed with Henri. Then his oldest brother was trampled to death in a street riot where they hanged another unfortunate baker because his bread prices were high. His other brother was shot by a guard when he tried to steal some bread for us to eat.

Dr. Curtius closed his exhibit to keep gangs of people from breaking in to destroy the wax statues of the royal figures they despise. That put Henri out of a job. For a while, the money Papa gave me sustained us, but one night I discovered that the small purse I had carried in the pocket of my dress was not there. I'd been pickpocketed! Henri and I were soon on the street, homeless.

I'm not sure who has it worse, Ernestine or me. Just as she is a prisoner of the revolutionaries, I am a prisoner of the streets.

Most of my days are spent fishing through garbage for food. Once in a while I find work sweeping out a store or cleaning up in a café. Some days I beg.

As often as I can, I come to the Tuileries and watch my family in the courtyard inside. How I miss them all!

*　　*　　*

Today, as Ernestine walks in the Tuileries courtyard, I mingle with the crowd that hounds her from behind the fence. Louis-Charles seems to be in his own world as he sits nearby reading. He doesn't look well. Thank goodness he has our governess, Madame de Tourzel, to look after him.

Aunt Élisabeth sketches on the ground with a piece of charcoal. Mama and Papa seem saddest of all as they stroll together, talking quietly, their heads bowed. Ernestine is the only one brave enough to come close to the crowd, which jeers at her. She's so regal one would never guess she wasn't born to it. It's because she comes so near, that we see each other.

Our eyes meet, though she gives me only the merest flicker of acknowledgment. I barely recognize her; she's grown so thin and pale. She's still pretty, though, in her white muslin dress with the blue sash and her beautiful blonde hair flowing freely down to her waist. How sad she looks.

I never stay long because I'm too scared that someone will notice the resemblance between Ernestine and me. It's probably an empty fear since our differing circumstances have made us dissimilar: she so delicate and frail-looking, yet lovely; me dirty, disheveled, and bug-eyed with hunger.

Out here in the streets I see things that I wish with all my heart I had never witnessed. Just weeks ago the prisons were besieged by a mob that tore open the cells of those jailed for being loyal to the royals. I saw women with ears pinned to their dresses, dismembered limbs lying in the road. The gutters ran red with blood.

I stood in the street and watched a cart with the carnage piled in the back and I began to cry. A man approached me wearing a kindly expression. "This is a terrible business," he said, "but they are our deadly enemies, and those who are delivering the country from them are saving your life and the lives of all the dear children of France."

I don't know what to say to him. How could this misery and horror save anyone? Could his words really be true?

And still, I am lucky. No one threatens to kill me. I'm free to go where I want. It's not right that Ernestine took my place. I didn't think so when it was proposed, and I still don't think it's fair. I have to find a way to get in, to be with my family.

Henri comes to find me. "Want to go to the Place de la Concorde?" he asks.

No. I don't. But I go with him because he wants to see if Mademoiselle Grosholtz is among those being beheaded that day. They've held her in prison for months and months now, but every day could be her last. Henri has learned that Dr. Curtius is trying to have her freed but with no success.

"Why must we go to the guillotine every single day?" I complain. I can't stand to see the people killed, and yet the crowd can't get enough of it. The Place de la Concorde is always mobbed with cheering "citizens." Now they call it Place de la Révolution, which only makes me despise it all the more.

But Henri insists on going. He says that if Mademoiselle is doomed, our presence will comfort her.

"Why do you care so much about Mademoiselle?" I ask him, thinking of her unsmiling face, her severe, frightening manner.

"She's all the family I have left," Henri explains after a thoughtful moment. "She saw I was starving and hired me. The money I earned saved me and my brothers' lives at that time. I'm not a person to forget that kindness."

"And yet this revolution that you believe in will kill her for no reason," I challenge. "Whose side are you on?"

My voice rises, and some in the crowd turn to look at us.

"I believe in the Revolution!" Henri shouts. He stares meaningfully at me. "Just as you, too, believe in the Revolution. Long live the Revolution!"

I realize his show is for the benefit of those around us, and I try to force a smile but my attempt fails.

People nod and wave their arms in the air. "To the Revolution!" some echo.

Henri grabs my arm and leans in close. "Do you want to get us killed?" he hisses softly. "Cheer the Revolution."

Opening my mouth, the words won't come.

Henri shakes me.

I break free of him, running into the crowd, tears running down my face. This thing threatens to destroy all I love.

I *hate* the Revolution! Despise it!

Blinded by my tears, I stumble into an alley and trip over a bundle lying in my path. I've tripped over a woman wrapped in rags, a baby on her lap. Her dirty hair is matted, and the languid child is also filthy.

"I'm sorry," I apologize, regaining my balance.

"Have you any food for my baby?" the woman croaks. "My milk has dried up."

"I don't, nor money, either," I reply honestly. A picture of the royal kitchen flashes in my head: the smell of newly made tarts being pulled from the oven, the roasted game birds, the savory scent of casseroles and stews. I gave them no special attention when I lived at the palace. How my mouth waters for that luscious food now! I would gladly share it with this ragged woman and her hungry baby.

The baby begins to whimper, and I can't stand the pitiful look on its face. Looking around, I see people on the street. "Wait," I say. "I'll get some food or money for you."

Returning to the street, I look around for a well-dressed person to approach. There are few to be found. These days it's dangerous to come out looking even a little well off. A person of affluence might be set upon by a mob merely for seeming to be middle-class. Finally, though, a man in a brocade jacket and velvet breeches comes into view. "Can you spare some money for a poor beggar?" I implore him.

"Go away, beggar girl," he snarls, hurrying past me.

"But her baby is starving," I say, trailing behind.

"Whose baby? I see no baby," the man snaps irritably.

"There's a woman in the alley," I say pivoting back to point. When I turn to face the man once more, he has walked off.

I approach each well-dressed person who comes along, begging for something to give this baby, and am ignored or pushed away time and again. One woman even kicks me for daring to talk to her.

"Curse you!" I shout at her, infuriated, shaking my fist. "I hope someday you starve the way that baby starves now!"

That's when I hear the fury of the crowd reflected in my own outburst — the rage, the frustration. It's so unfair! Why should some have so much while others get nothing?

The world shifts for me in that moment. I see myself, Madame Royale, and my entire family, as the people of France see us, and my stomach clenches.

How they must hate us. How they *do* hate us. And I suddenly understand why.

But my parents didn't create the world they were born into. The world of kings and queens wasn't their invention. It's been this way for centuries. Have other royal families done a better job of it?

It's more than I can understand.

Now that I've had an experience of the deep anger and truly felt it, the emotion terrifies me. I'm stunned by it.

Finally, I sit on a curb, miserable, defeated.

After a while I see Henri searching for me and call to him. I tell him what I've been doing and he pulls a chunk of bread from the pocket of his pants. "Give her this. I stole it from a woman's market basket," he reveals.

"You stole it?" I ask. Begging is bad enough. But stealing?

He shrugs. Heading back into the alley with Henri following, I look around for the woman and her baby, but they aren't there anymore.

Ernestine tried to warn me. You don't want to see the real France, she insisted, but I had no idea of what she meant. How I wish I still didn't.

$\mathcal{C}$HAPTER 12

$\mathcal{D}$ay after day we watch the guillotine. Mademoiselle Grosholtz doesn't appear at the Place de la Révolution, but many other people do.

I wish that I could wipe the beheadings from my memory.

Today the crowd pushes us closer than usual, right up front. I recognize the first victim, a woman who runs an umbrella stand at the Palais-Royal. She's charged with spying for the king and queen. She is tied to a plank with her hands trussed behind the piece of wood, and then lowered so that her neck is directly below the blade.

Henri and I stand in front, and I cast my eyes downward, not wanting to make eye contact with the terrified woman who glances around wildly, desperate for someone to come forward who can save her from this awful fate.

The blade falls with a terrible *thunk*. It makes me jump, and for a second I don't realize that Henri and I have both been spattered in a hot, red spray.

But then I taste the iron-tinged sweetness of blood on my lips. It's in my hair. On my hands.

My horror rises.

In the crowd around me, some cheer, others laugh. The woman's head rolls to the ground in front of the guillotine, leaving a trail of red before it settles.

My disgust and fear race through my body like a runaway wagon, and I vomit. Repulsed by the stench of the bile spewing from me, those nearby jump away.

Wiping my mouth with my sleeve, I straighten to see a thin young man, not too much older than me, being tied to the plank, the next to be beheaded.

Head after severed head lands in a pile at the base of the guillotine. My horror lessens with each death. Something is dying inside me, becoming dull and hard. I don't like the sensation, but it enables me to tolerate this and so I let the internal callousness grow without a struggle.

At night Henri and I snuggle on a park bench, staying close as much from a need to stay warm as from affection. Henri holds my hand, saying nothing, until I fall asleep.

"How can you stand it?" I ask him one night.

"It's for the freedom of France," he says, but his voice trails up at the end of his sentence, as if it's more of a question than a statement.

"Even freedom can't possibly be worth all this, can it?" I ask.

"I don't know," he admits. "When I see the aristocracy as a group, they seem evil to me, enemies of the working and impoverished citizens of France. When I think of an individual like Mademoiselle Grosholtz being killed, it doesn't seem right."

The next morning, Henri finds us a croissant to split for our breakfast. I no longer ask where he gets the food.

"I want to go to the exhibit this morning to see if it's been reopened," he tells me, nibbling at the flaky bread to make it last longer. "Maybe I can find work there again."

We go to Dr. Curtius's exhibit and find it dark and padlocked. "I have a key to the back workroom," Henri says, already heading for it. He opens the door and we enter.

Mademoiselle Grosholtz stands beside a small stove, stirring a pot of melting wax.

I stagger, wide-eyed, disbelieving my own eyes. How can this be?

"You've escaped!" Henri cries.

Something akin to a smile plays across Mademoiselle's pale, serious face. "Not entirely. Uncle Philippe — Dr. Curtius — knows a man who has influence with the revolutionaries.

"He finally convinced them that I'm not dangerous and that I am more useful to them alive than dead," she goes on, still stirring her pot of wax. She scrutinizes me but says nothing.

Henri takes a seat at a long wooden worktable and I sit beside him. "What will you do for them?" he asks.

Mademoiselle's attention is diverted by a woman she sees lingering outside the upper window of the back door. "Rose," she cries softly and a glint of happiness lights those steely eyes as she hurries to let the woman enter.

Rose appears tall, though she is not much bigger than Mademoiselle. Rather, she is regal, square shouldered, and lithe, with her tumble of black curls gathered in gold cord atop her head. Perfectly arched black brows frame eyes like sparking coals, and a softly curving mouth tips up on both sides into something like a permanently amused smile. To me she's like a goddess from another world as she shrugs off her feather-trimmed burgundy velvet coat.

"My dear friend, it's been too long," Mademoiselle Grosholtz says, her voice a warm caress of sincerity. "How have you been since last I saw you?" Her solicitude makes me believe that these two have shared some terrible ordeal, awful suffering.

Rose's smile bends into chagrin. "Not well, I'm afraid. They are still holding Alexandre. The Revolutionary Guard decided that he was attached somehow to the royals just because he is wealthy."

Mademoiselle gasps. "Your poor husband! I'm so happy that they didn't keep you, as well. How did you get away?"

"If it were not for the gallantry and influence of Dr. Curtius and some of his friends, I might well have been beheaded."

Suddenly, I know where I've seen Rose — in the prison cart that day with Mademoiselle.

"How did you keep your hair?" I blurt, and immediately blush with embarrassment. I know that those headed for the guillotine have their hair shorn to be sold for wigs. It seems such a frivolous question, though. But, still, I am dazzled by the luxuriant raven curls that are piled atop her head.

Rose throws her head back, laughing at my impulsivity before she answers. "I convinced them that the longer they let it grow on my head, the more money they'd get for the wig. I persuaded them so well that I think they might have kept my severed head just for the curls growing from it."

Rose studies the effect her words were having on me. How was I receiving the grotesque tale? Was I being tested? "Hair grows even after one is dead, you know," she adds.

"I wasn't as lucky," Mademoiselle says, pulling off her cap to reveal a nearly bald skull. Shutting her eyes, a tremble runs through her, as though recalling the terrifying moment when she must have been certain she was destined for the guillotine's blade. "I didn't have your lovely curls to bargain with," Mademoiselle adds.

"Oh, you had something much better," Rose insists as she settles into a chair by the table. "Your skills! Your wax faces!"

"Thankfully you were there to think of it," Mademoiselle says. "It gave Dr. Curtius something to offer the brutes. But now I must pay the gruesome price."

"What price is that?" Henri asks.

"I've been ordered by the revolutionary regime to collect the heads of people of note who are guillotined."

"Why?" I cry, horrified.

"Death masks," Mademoiselle reveals glumly.

I recall Henri telling me about death masks. "That's horrible," I mutter.

"Where will you make them?" Henri asks. "Here?"

"Here," Mademoiselle confirms. "I'll need your help, Henri, and that of your friend there." Mademoiselle Grosholtz focuses on me once more. "I know you from the palace . . . don't I?"

I feel like a trapped animal. Frozen and unaware of what to do next.

How do I answer? This is a woman who studies faces, remembers the details. She's already rendered my face in wax — twice! Once as Marie-Thérèse-Charlotte sitting at the royal table, and then again the evening that I sat across from her at the servants' table.

"You're the maid's daughter," Mademoiselle says, "the one who so strongly resembles Madame Royale."

"Yes," I agree quickly, struggling to stay composed, not to let my relief show. "They call me Ernestine."

"That's an ugly name," Mademoiselle remarks, eyes still locked onto my face. "Is it your real name?"

I shake my head. "My true name is Marie-Thérèse, like the princess. That's why the queen nicknamed me Ernestine. It was after a character in a novel she was reading."

"Every female in France is named Marie," Rose says. "My name is Marie Rose de Beauharnais, though my given name is Marie-

Josèphe-Rose Tascher de La Pagerie. Mademoiselle Grosholtz is Anna Marie. We have to call ourselves by other names or there would be mass confusion." This strikes her as funny and she laughs.

"What's the difference what we're called?" I ask lightly, wanting to keep the merriness afloat.

"It matters very much," Rose says with a sharp new solemnity. "Your name is at the heart of things."

"What things?" Henri asks.

Rose's eyes narrow at him. "I was born on the island of Martinique in the Caribbean Ocean," Rose says after a moment. Her voice has lowered and taken on a dark, distant tone.

"My parents were Creole plantation owners who had turned on their own kind and kept slaves to work the sugar crop," she continues. "Their treachery and disloyalty to their own people mortified me, and I wanted to escape them as much as the slaves did. At night I would steal away from the plantation and watch the slaves practice the magical ways that they'd brought with them from their homes in Africa. A priestess made me her apprentice and taught me her ways of getting to the heart of the magic ways of the spirits and the dead."

I shiver listening to her words. Rose seems to vibrate with a power that emanates from her very being.

"What did she teach you?" I dare to ask.

"You wouldn't understand," Mademoiselle says with force. Despite her harshness, I sense that she's protecting me from some unpleasantness.

Rose disregards her and continues, "The first thing I learned was to work with roots and herbs."

"To do what with them?" Henri asks.

"Potions, poisons, spells," Rose replies.

"Did you ever poison someone?" Henri is eager to know.

"I never did it myself, but I've seen it done," Rose says. "I saw a man who had toyed with the affections of a voodoo priestess turned into a zombie. She used the poison from a certain fish. The poison paralyzed all his organs and made him seem to be dead, and he was buried alive. By the dark of night his body was exhumed and he was brought back. From then on he was a zombie, a mindless creature, and for the rest of his days, he served the voodoo priestess he had wronged."

"What else can you do?" Henri asks, rapt with fascination.

"You don't need to know these things," Mademoiselle interjects. "There's work to be done. We're going to the Place de la Révolution."

"Why there?" I ask, suddenly sickened by the thought.

Mademoiselle Grosholtz nods at her basket. "We will sort through the pile and collect the severed heads of the famous and the beautiful."

Alarmed, I look to Henri. Is she serious?

He stares back, his eyebrows raised as if to ask, *Would you rather starve?*

This time I know it isn't a test.

CHAPTER 13

O n the first day of our hideous new assignment, I don the bonnet rouge, the red cap of the revolutionaries, as do Henri and Mademoiselle Grosholtz. Mademoiselle says that if we wear them as well as the tricolor ribbon, no one will stop us as we select heads from among those piled in front of the guillotine.

We arrive at the crowded Place de la Révolution. It's already crowded with people who want to witness this horror. The people — or I should say *Citizens*, for now everyone is an equal *Citizen* of France, and is to be addressed as such — all chatter about how the guillotine is a much more humane way to die than being hung or shot. They seem proud to be murdering their fellow citizens in such a merciful way.

I hang back and watch Mademoiselle Grosholtz charge through the mob. "Make way! Make way!" she shouts to part the gathered crowd. "By order of the National Convention, I have come to collect the heads of the dead."

Henri stands midway between me and Mademoiselle, as though filled with divided loyalty. With a small gesture, he signals for me to come forward. But I can't.

In that pile I might find the heads of soldiers who have been kind to me, servants I know and love, advisers and ministers I've seen at the palace many times. How can I stand to look?

Luckily, Mademoiselle and Henri don't insist that I join them, but get on with their horrendous work. Mademoiselle sorts through the heads as though she is looking for the best cabbage at the market. Henri gazes into the sunny sky but holds the basket steadily as Mademoiselle picks up each head she selects and places it carefully inside the basket.

It's a warm day, and the stench of rotting bodies is becoming overwhelming. Sitting on the street curb, I cradle my head in my hands to keep from fainting or puking.

At first, the babble of the crowd is just a garble of voices to me as I concentrate on breathing steadily. But slowly I discern the secretive tones of two women speaking together just a few feet away.

"Tonight we plant the Liberty Trees," a short, sloppy redhead says, and her voice is loaded with meaning.

The other woman chortles with malice. "We'll plant a nice tree right at the front gate of the Tuileries Palace, won't we?"

"It's a tree they'll never forget," the redhead says.

They're talking about more than planting trees. I'm sure of it. They're planning something.

"They've lived in luxury long enough," the redhead adds. "It's much too cozy in there, if you ask me."

Her friend grins. "I couldn't agree more." The two put their heads together and continue laughing.

They're talking about my family! What's happening? What do they intend to do? I have to find out.

"Pardon me," I say, slowing rising from the curb. "Do you need more helpers for the tree planting tonight?"

The women stare at me warily. "Are you a friend of the French people?" one of them asks.

The woman's redheaded friend punches her arm. "Don't be stupid! Look at the red cap, the tricolor ribbon."

"Are you loyal to the Revolution?" the dark-haired woman asks me. "Do you understand all that it means? Are you old enough to join the French people in their fight tonight?"

"Of course I'm loyal," I say. "I'm loyal enough and old enough to plant a tree."

The dark-haired woman leans toward me. "Are you old enough to kill a queen?" she whispers.

Mademoiselle Grosholtz makes beds for Henri and me in the workroom of the exhibit. They are just two planks with blankets and pillows, and a curtain hung between them for privacy. Though they're hard, they are better than sleeping on a park bench or the ground as Henri and I have done so often.

"Good night, Henri," I say from my side of the curtain. "Sleep well."

"Good night, Ernestine."

"Henri, you know how much you mean to me, don't you?"

Henri peeks around the curtain. "What is it?"

I sit up and pull my knees to my chest as he crosses to my side of the room. "Nothing."

"I can tell something is wrong," he says.

"Things are just so uncertain these days," I say. "I want you to know how much you mean to me."

Henri scrutinizes me with serious eyes. "It was the severed heads today, wasn't it? I know how upset you were."

"How could you bring yourself to do it?" I blurt. "How could you?"

Henri shakes his head. "I don't know. Mademoiselle Grosholtz needed the help."

Impulsively, I lean forward and squeeze his arm. "It's all so horrible!"

He sits on the edge of the bed and hugs me close. I place my head on his shoulder and breathe deeply. For a moment the world goes away and I feel safe. It's just Henri and me in our own private universe. Turning his head, Henri kisses my lips gently. I'm happy my first kiss is from him because I love him so much.

Am I *in love* with Henri? I don't know. I've never been in love. I only know he's my dearest friend besides Ernestine, and he's been so good to me. When we're together, I feel I'm with someone who wants only the best for me and to protect me as much as is possible. When we're parted, I just want to get back to him. If I see something lovely, I wish he were there to see it, too. Is that love? I think it could be. "If we're ever parted, we'll find each other," I say, "no matter how long it takes."

"Yes, we will," he agrees.

"Promise?"

"Promise."

He lays his head back on my pillow, and it isn't long before his eyes drift shut. I wait until his breathing turns heavy and I know he's asleep, then I get up and kiss his forehead lightly, hoping he will be able to forgive me for what I'm about to do.

How can I leave him? It feels like such treachery. But I have to rejoin my family. I will find my way back to him. I promise myself that.

Silently, I dress and slip out of the workshop. I suspect that the Tuileries Palace is about to come under siege. It could be my one and only chance to ever rejoin my family.

All over Paris the streets are lit with torches as people plant trees around the city. There's a feeling of celebration, like a giant party. People sing songs of liberty. They drink, too: wine, beer, every kind of alcohol. It's not long before the city is a raucous assemblage of drunken revelers.

Maybe nothing sinister is happening, I think. Perhaps it's just a night of parties and tree planting. My feelings are mixed, because it means my family is safe but also that my plans to go back to them are not going to happen.

I move along with the crowd and as it nears the Tuileries Palace, the mood shifts. The songs filling the night air become more hostile, filthy, and aggressive. Brawls break out among the intoxicated people. Smaller groups from all over the city converge at the gates of the palace until it is one giant mob.

"Let us in!" a woman shouts at the guard in front.

Remembering the attack at Versailles, I know these people will break in one way or another. Therefore I'm not entirely surprised that the guard unlocks the gate and steps aside. He's not going to get killed to protect my family. The days of that sort of loyalty are gone.

A roar wells up as the people surge forward through the open gates. The saws, axes, picks, and shovels used for planting trees are suddenly brandished as weapons. I'm terrified by the fury of the mob, but there's no turning back as I'm swept along in the frenzy.

I'm practically lifted off my feet, pushed forward by the wave of people on every side. Will I even be able to find my family before these people do? I suddenly wonder what I could possibly have been thinking to come here tonight.

CHAPTER 14

*T*hough I've never lived at the Tuileries for any length of time, I've visited and know its secret passages. As the savage mob races down a hallway, brutalizing any servants who stand in their way, I search for a certain closet door. When I see it, I step inside.

"Where is she going?" I hear a woman ask, and I freeze with fear.

"Leave her," someone answers. "She's hiding in the closet. The poor dope is scared."

That's certainly true! Pushing aside capes and coats, I run my hand along the wall and find the latch I seek. Pushing through the door, I face a curving stone staircase and race upward. I'm breathless by the time I burst into Mama's chambers.

Madame de Tourzel sits reading to Louis-Charles while Ernestine writes in a journal and Aunt Élisabeth sketches. Obviously, they haven't yet realized what's happening down below.

Mama sits in a chair, engrossed in her needlework. Looking up casually, she pales and drops her work when she sees me.

They all stand in alarm, shocked, as though I'm a ghost.

There's no time for explanations or endearments. "Come on! Into the passage. Quickly!" I say. "There is a mob headed right for you."

Without a word, they hurry into the secret passage. I'm the last out and I make sure the door is shut tightly, locked behind me.

"This way," Mama directs us. Apparently, she's also no stranger to these tunnels. It's very dark but we keep hold of one another, making a chain of clasped hands as we hurry on. "Wait here," she commands us. Light shines through a doorway I'd never have known was there, and she quickly returns with Papa, dressed for bed, and his personal valet, Monsieur Cléry. In the darkness Papa doesn't see me, but he bids farewell to his servant before leading the way onward.

As we travel through the tunnel, I hear muted screams and shouts. The walls vibrate with the violence I know is happening in the hallways and rooms. Are the guards fighting the crowd? Are there any left who would bother? What's happening to the servants and other nobles still in the palace? I can't let myself think about it or I'll become paralyzed with terror.

We reach the passageway's end and pour into a very small chamber containing only a cabinet, three velvet-backed chairs, and an elegant but faded rug. There are no windows. Papa bolts the door behind us. Mama takes a chair and Louis-Charles climbs into her lap, burying his face in her shoulder. Ernestine and I huddle together on the rug. Papa and Aunt Élisabeth sit side by side on the chairs while Madame de Tourzel sits on the floor in a corner, cradling her head in her hands.

The screams outside the room have heightened, punctuated with outbursts of malicious laughter. I hear gunshots. Things crash and shatter as furniture is smashed into walls. Ernestine bows her head and covers her ears to block it all out.

"Don't be scared," I say to comfort Ernestine, although it's a foolish thing to say. We are all terrified.

Ernestine lifts her head and we look at each other, our expressions alive with emotion. Her eyes are reproachful, questioning. What am I doing here? Why did I return on such an awful night? But she must know that I came in order to save them, to save all of us.

Little Louis-Charles slides to the floor and begins to sob. Mama rubs his back and cradles him in her skirts, to muffle the sound of his crying as well as to comfort him.

Mama stretches out her free hand and clasps mine. Papa, too, casts a warm look my way. How happy I am to see them again — all of them! We all long to speak, but it's a time for silence and no one dares.

The agonizing night lasts an eternity. But, finally, there's quiet.

"Can we go back to our rooms?" Ernestine asks.

Papa shakes his head and whispers in reply, "It could be a trap. We'll stay put a little longer."

"Marie-Thérèse, come hug your mother," Mama says, which I do as she holds me tight. I kiss Louis-Charles, too. How big he's grown since I last saw him, though he seems too thin. All of them look haggard and worn.

"You should go soon," Papa says to me. "You don't want to call attention to yourself by leaving here alone."

"I'm staying," I insist firmly.

"No, you're not," Ernestine says with equal conviction.

"You can't," Papa agrees. "They don't know about Ernestine. They're not looking for her. If they find the two of you here, they will know we've been deceiving them."

"Then let Ernestine go," I say. "She's been in here long enough. It's not fair. Besides, I miss you all so much."

"And we miss you," Mama says. "We pray for your safety every night. Did your uncle come for you?"

I shake my head. "What happened to his army?"

Mama sighs. "You don't hear any talk of an approaching force from Austria?"

"Nothing," I say.

Mama and Papa look at each other sadly. I feel as though I've just dashed their last hope.

"So you've been on your own all this time?" Mama asks.

I tell them about Henri and Mademoiselle Grosholtz. They're relieved to know I have friends and a place to stay. I need to convince them that Ernestine will be comfortable enough in my place, with friends to look out for her.

"People saw me come in dressed in these clothes, so we'll have to switch outfits," I say, acting as though it's been settled and Ernestine is going to leave. "I'll give you the address to find Henri. He's at Dr. Curtius's exhibit. The exhibit is shut down but go around the back and —"

"I'm not going, Marie-Thérèse. As you just saw tonight, you're safer out there than you are in here." I can see from her firm expression that Ernestine will not be convinced otherwise.

Papa stands and puts his hand on my shoulder. "Marie-Thérèse, you owe it to France to stay away. Hopefully, we will all be together again before long. Something has delayed them, but Austria may yet come to our aide. You must be available to rally them to our cause, to show we are still a force in France."

I mean him no disrespect, but I have to laugh. "Look at me, Papa," I say, spreading my arms wide. "Do I look like someone a foreign king or queen would rally behind? I'm a beggar girl."

"I see a Bourbon princess," he says. "I see Marie-Thérèse-Charlotte, Madame Royale of France, a lovely young woman yet still the Child of France."

His faith and pride in me makes a sob catch in my throat. I want to be worthy of his trust, but it's so difficult.

There's a tap on the door, and we all freeze. But then we hear the voice of Monsieur Cléry. "Your Highness, the crowd is gone. The National Assembly has ordered all of us to report to their headquarters. They've sent carriages and guards to escort us there."

Papa opens the door to him, and we all stand, preparing to leave. Monsieur Cléry's grooming is usually impeccable, so we all stare with concern at his disheveled appearance. Not only are his clothes torn and his eye blackened, but his powdered wig, which I've never seen him without, is altogether gone, revealing a bald head.

Aware of our unspoken questions, he wrings his hands. "I don't think you want to see what is back at the palace," he states solemnly, "especially not the young dauphin. It could scar him for life."

"Are you all right, Monsieur?" Mama asks him.

For a moment, an expression of wild panic flashes across his face, and then he regains his composure. "Quite all right," he says, clearly lying. "I know a passage that will bring us to the back courtyard, and I've directed the carriages to be brought there. The maids who have survived are packing right now and —"

"Those that survived?" Mama interrupts, her face pale.

"Yes, Your Highness. Forgive me. We must hurry or the National Assembly will grow impatient."

Madame de Tourzel takes Louis-Charles from Mama's arms and heads for the door. "You two really are like twins," she remarks to Ernestine and me. I squeeze Ernestine into a quick affectionate hug.

"Come, girls," Mama says from the door. "Hurry."

I'm cheered that they're including me in their entourage, but when I'm about to step out of the doorway and go to one of the two waiting carriages, Mama squeezes my shoulder to stop my progress.

"Go back to your friends and stay safe," she says. "It's better that way. Now that we know where you are, we can find you when all this awfulness ends."

I throw my arms around her, desperate to stay with my family, and she holds me tightly. "Will it ever end?" I ask her. This insanity has been going on for so long. Maybe it won't end. Perhaps this is how life will be from now on. The people have turned into savages, beasts, and they'll prey on my family until they devour them completely.

"Of course it will end," Mama assures me. "These things always end. The American Revolution ended." She smiles wryly. "Even the Hundred Years' War ended eventually."

"A hundred years of this!" I cry, horrified at the idea.

"No! No!" she says, patting my back. "That was a foolish joke. By this time next year, we'll all be together again. Perhaps not Paris, maybe in Austria, but somewhere."

"Your Highness, you must go," Monsieur Cléry urges.

"What about you and the rest of the serving staff?" Mama asks him.

"The servants are to remain here to await further instruction from the National Assembly."

"Very well," Mama agrees, though this news seems to worry her. She frees herself from my grip and presses a green velvet purse into my hands. "Hide it," she whispers. "Use the coins to live. Keep the jewels for bribery and survival," she adds as she hurries out into the night. Immediately, two members of the Revolutionary Guard flank her, not noticing me hanging back in the shadowy doorway.

Monsieur Cléry draws me back farther. "They mustn't see you."

Naturally, he's right, but still I strain forward, aching for a last view of my family as the carriages rattle out of the courtyard. How long will it be until I see my beloved family and friends again?

CHAPTER 15

Monsieur Cléry guides me stealthily around the palace walls with an unsteady grip on my arm. "What will the National Assembly do to them?" I ask.

"I don't know," Monsieur Cléry says, but I suspect he knows more than he's willing to tell.

"Is everyone inside dead?" I dare to ask.

"Nearly," he admits. "Some of us were able to hide in the passageways." He stops, trembling all over, covering his eyes with his hands. "Anything they didn't steal, they destroyed. They ransacked the palace and killed anyone in their path. Even the guards were no match for their ferocity. They were a pack of rabid dogs." I notice for the first time that there's a wide smear of blood across the back of his jacket. I don't have the nerve to ask how it got there.

When we reach the wide avenue leading to the palace, I'm happy to see that it's nearly deserted, though farther off in the city I still hear revelry and see the flares of bonfires. "Keep to the backstreets," Monsieur Cléry advises. "In the coming days you might consider darkening your hair, to make it harder for that horde to recognize you."

·"Thank you for all you have done for my family," I say.

"Your parents are good people, dignified and strong," he replies, choking a little with emotion. "It is my honor to serve them."

After all the insults, lies, and jeers, it's so soothing to hear a kind word. Tears of gratitude well in my eyes. Monsieur Cléry notices them and sighs. "Your Highness, you are the bravest young woman I have ever met. I am proud to know you."

"Thank you, Monsieur," I say. "I'll try to live up to your idea of who I am."

Turning, I head down the wide avenue of Tuileries Park, which is lit only with an occasional lantern hanging from a pole and the beams of a luminous full moon. I veer to the right side, where the tulip beds that have just recently begun to sprout have been trampled by the marauding crowd.

Tossed in a bush, illuminated by the moon, is one of Mama's pink silk shawls. Thinking I would like to have something of hers, I step off the path to retrieve it but recoil when I touch it. It's soaked in blood!

What kind of horrible massacre went on in there?!

The dark silhouette of a male figure has stepped off the path and is approaching. Panic seizes me. Every muscle tenses. "Get back!" I shout. "I have a gun. I stole it from the palace tonight." It's a lie, but maybe it will frighten him.

"Ernestine. It's me. I've been looking for you all night."

"Henri!" I cry, sagging with relief as he reaches me.

"Do you really have a gun?" he asks softly.

I lean on his shoulder, so happy to see him. "No. I don't have a gun, but I was in the palace."

"I heard it was a . . . very bad. Are you all right?"

"The screaming and fighting — it went on for hours. We hid in a small, secret room. If they'd found us . . ." I shudder, thinking of what might have happened.

"We?" he questions. "Who were you hiding with?"

In my distress, I've said too much. Henri and I face each other, speechless.

But then, Henri puts his arm around me and guides me to a dark, secluded bench, and we sit together. "Ernestine," he says in a low, sincere tone. "You listen to me now." I've never before heard him sound so serious.

"What is it?"

"I know who you are; who you *really* are."

My breath catches in surprise.

"Why didn't you tell me yourself?" His voice is accusing, hurt. "Don't you trust me?"

"I trust you, but it's a secret that could have gotten you killed." I shut my eyes for a moment as I recall the boy, just a little older than me, we saw beheaded that day in the Place de la Révolution. What if that happened to Henri because he was discovered helping me? Nothing could help him then, not all the red caps or tricolor ribbons in all of France.

"How long have you known?"

"I told you before that I noticed the resemblance when I first compared your face to that of the wax princess in the exhibit. But later you said you looked like the princess, so I chose to believe you."

"The real Ernestine does look almost exactly like me."

"Then, tonight," he continues, "Mademoiselle Grosholtz was talking to Rose in the workroom and I heard what they were saying. She told Rose that she was certain you were Marie-Thérèse-Charlotte."

Gasping with alarm, my hand flies across my gaping mouth. Can they be trusted? Will they turn me in for a reward?

"Don't worry. They won't tell. They both hate the revolutionaries," Henri says. "They were imprisoned, remember? Rose's husband is still in jail for being a royalist, and Mademoiselle was almost guillotined — she was only days away from it."

His words calm me down some. "I'm sorry I didn't tell you, Henri. Honestly, I am. I'll never lie to you again. I promise."

"Then tell me, Ernest —" He cuts himself short. "I mean Princess Marie-Thérèse, what —"

"Shhh!" I hiss, looking around frantically. There are spies everywhere these days. "You see why I couldn't tell you?" I whisper fiercely. "What if you'd been overheard just now?"

"You're right," he agrees. "I'm sorry. That was stupid of me. I'll keep calling you Ernestine. What were you planning to do out here tonight? Why were you in the palace? You could have been killed. Were you going to leave without even saying good-bye to me?"

"That's what I was trying to tell you tonight — that I'd find a way to get back to you. Didn't you understand that?"

We sit silently beside each other and watch as the sky becomes gray with predawn light. Henri laces his fingers into mine and I squeeze his hand. It's good to be quiet together, comforting.

CHAPTER 16

*S*ix months pass and what a strange time it is!

Day in and day out, Henri and I travel to the Place de la Révolution with Mademoiselle Grosholtz and climb among the pile of heads searching for the best ones: the most famous, the most beautiful, the most interesting.

The crowd recognizes us by now and parts to let us through. We're there on the authority of the Terror, what the revolutionaries are calling their regime now. They're well named, as everyone in Paris fears them.

Because we're emissaries of the Revolutionary Tribunal, those who run the Terror, no one dares to get in our way. And the strange thing is that I find an odd pleasure in playing the part: scowling, glaring; once I realized I was even baring my teeth. Ernestine the terrible ragamuffin, not to be toyed with, nor taken lightly — a fierce animal of the streets.

A terrorist!

Look at me the wrong way, and you might be the next to have your head chopped off! I can arrange it.

In my old role as the Royal Child of France, I wouldn't ever dare be this imperious. This charade is so ridiculous it makes me want to laugh out loud, but I don't dare. My acting is deadly serious business. It keeps everyone back and looking away, from studying my face too closely.

My pretend ferocity also distracts me from the task at hand.

We're sprayed with blood as each new head falls.

The ferocity of this new character I pretend to be helps me to overcome my revulsion. It's not me, Marie-Thérèse-Charlotte, watching the beheadings, but some other tougher, more unfeeling person. Just the same, I don't look at the severed heads any more than necessary. I don't *think* any more than necessary. I move in a sort of mindless state, like the zombies Rose de Beauharnais described to us.

Back at the workshop, Mademoiselle shuts the staring eyes of the dead and covers the faces in oil, then, hours before they stiffen, smears them in plaster to make an imprint of the face. She gently lifts off the dried plaster and then lets the hot wax on her burner cool somewhat before pouring it into the face mold she's created.

When members of the Revolutionary Guard arrive to collect the masks, they treat Mademoiselle Grosholtz rudely, reminding her that if she doesn't do her job well, she'll be thrown back into prison . . . or worse. Mademoiselle is stiffly polite to them. In some cases, the guards want the severed heads, too. They want to display the most famous heads atop high fences around Paris.

One day, a guard I recognize stares at me as I sew black human hair into a wig for the figure of Cleopatra in the exhibit. It takes a minute, but I recall seeing him last year as we were escorted back to Tuileries from Varennes.

I grow nauseated with worry and turn my head away from him. Has he recognized me? What will he do?

"Who is that girl?" he demands of Mademoiselle Grosholtz.

Mademoiselle is wrapping heads in cloth and piling them into the canvas bag the guards have brought. She continues with her task, never looking at me or the guard. "She's a beggar girl who has worked for me for the last four years, since she was twelve years old."

"What's her name?"

"She doesn't have one. She's no one, like so many children who live on the streets of Paris. I call her Zero because she's nobody."

"Zero," the guard addresses me roughly.

I reluctantly stand, pretending to cower in order to shield my face. "Yes, sir."

"Address me as Citizen. We are all equal citizens of the New French Republic now, are we not?"

"Yes, Citizen," I amend.

He looks me over and I force myself not to bite my lip or tremble, and finally he leaves.

That night Mademoiselle presents me with a jar of the dark brown dye she uses for her wigs and commands me to use it. "Everyone knows the princess is blonde like her mother," she says. "That lovely flaxen hair could cost you your life."

"Thank you." I know she's right, remembering how Monsieur Cléry gave me the same advice. At least hair dye is better than ink.

"I suggest you cut it, too," Mademoiselle adds.

Cut my hair! It makes sense, but the idea is so upsetting. It would be like cutting away one of the last links to my mother. "Would you cut it for me?" I ask. "I think my hand will shake too much."

"Do you see all the work there is to do here?" she snaps angrily. "Do you think I have time to coif your hair?"

"No," I say meekly.

Henri has been standing in the doorway witnessing all this. "I'll cut it for you," he offers.

Mademoiselle Grosholtz seems about to protest, probably to say that she needs him to work. But she stops herself and returns to oiling the face of the head in her hands.

Henri is used to working with the wigs in the studio, so when he bobs my newly brown hair to chin length and cuts fringe on my forehead, his work is straight and even. "Do you like it?" he asks.

I'm not sure, though I know it's better than the mess I would have made of it. "I hardly recognize myself," I say, looking into the tall mirror we have propped against the wall.

He smiles at our reflections. "Isn't that the idea?"

"I suppose so," I agree. "But it's odd to appear so different from the person I've always been."

"I think you look very pretty."

"Really?" Swiveling, I look up at him.

"Very pretty," he repeats as he takes my hand in his and presses a kiss into my palm. The gesture is so loving and reassuring that my eyes mist up. Henri is so good to me. How could I ever live without him?

The time quickly passes as Henri and I continue assisting Mademoiselle Grosholtz with her work. I learn more from her every day and find I like working with the wax — smoothing it, forming it. The repetitious nature of the task gives me pleasure in that it distracts me from all my worries.

Mademoiselle also seems to enjoy the work. I can see her silently making artistic choices as she labors to re-create the glow of life her models enjoyed when they lived. Under her meticulous, tender care, the women look beautiful, and the men peaceful and strong. I wonder if it's her way of paying tribute to the dead, compensating for the lack of prayer and funeral their desecrated bodies never received.

Rose de Beauharnais arrives late every night after the work is done. Henri and I steal out of our beds to watch Mademoiselle with Rose in the workroom. We've found a section of rotted wood in the corner of an adjacent room that can be pulled out. By lying flat on the floor we can see most of what they're doing.

At night, Rose lets her lush curls down around her shoulders and works in a flowered, satin kimono. With her dark arched brows and shining otherworldly eyes, I think she's the most beautiful woman I've ever seen.

We see another side of Mademoiselle Grosholtz, too. Though she wears her usual plain dress, mobcap, and apron, her stern face is lit with excitement. Whatever they're working on thrills her.

Rose is, as Henri guessed, using roots and herbs. Every night she arrives with packets of them, each time reporting some new discovery. "I found an herbalist working by the Seine who was selling turmeric," she reports eagerly. One night she comes in elated to have made contact with a chemist who opened his healing supplies to her, providing bat wings, rat brains, and ferret tongue. "Now we can really get somewhere," she pronounces as she gleefully displays her new treasures to Mademoiselle.

But as much as Rose grinds her ingredients with a pestle in a mortar and is assisted by Mademoiselle Grosholtz, who chops, shreds, and boils at her side . . . in the end she shakes her head in disappointment.

What are they trying to accomplish? Whatever it is, success is eluding them. But each night they attempt it anew . . . setting out the ingredients, chanting over them . . .

And fail once more.

Until one night.

Henri and I watch, fascinated, as Rose boils her exotic potion and holds up a large, whole ginger root over the steam. The root looks so much like the figure of a little man. Then I realize that Mademoiselle has placed a small wax head on top of it, like the head she created of me so long ago.

As Rose holds the figure in the hot mist, she intones words I can't understand. It's a cross between speech and song — and she is deadly serious as she works her magic.

The next thing I see makes me doubt my own eyes.

Rose places the ginger-root creature upright on the table, but it doesn't topple over. My jaw drops in silent disbelief as the creature takes a faltering step forward! It takes another step and then another.

Finally, when it reaches the end of the table, it stumbles. Mademoiselle Grosholtz steadies it and then gently lifts it, cradling the creature in a cloth. Rose slumps into a chair, a look of triumph on her face.

Mademoiselle places the root creature in a cabinet and locks it. Then she and Rose hug, rapturous with delight.

At Henri's nod, we hastily stuff the rotted, mulchy wood back into the opening and look at each other, amazed. "You saw that, too, didn't you?" Henri asks, pale and wide-eyed.

"I did."

"After she goes to sleep, let's try to open that cabinet," he says.

Do we dare? How can we not? This strange creature is true magic! I've never even imagined something like this could exist.

Is it still alive? Can it speak? Why have they created it? What are they doing?

I'm in a fever of curiosity. I *must* explore this further.

"I'm good with locks," I tell Henri. Locks and keys are Papa's hobby, and he's shown me all about them.

"All right, then," Henri replies. "We'll wait for them to leave. As soon as they're gone we can sneak in."

But Mademoiselle stretches out on the worktable, fully dressed, and never goes to her room to sleep. Henri and I wait for hours until we fall asleep, lying there on the floor.

We check again just before dawn. Mademoiselle is no longer lying on the table. Eagerly, we hurry into the workroom. All it takes for me to get the cabinet lock open is one of the tiny, sharp-tipped awls Mademoiselle uses in her work.

But the cabinet is empty!

"Where is it?" Henri asks in a sharp whisper as he searches behind baskets and wooden boxes. I don't see the root creature. I'm so intent in our pursuit that Mademoiselle Grosholtz's presence startles me, and Henri and I whirl to face her.

Mademoiselle carries a large willow basket. Whatever is in it is covered in a small blanket. "How did you unlock that?" she asks.

I hold up the tool.

"We needed a nail to make the eye pupils on those heads we built yesterday," Henri lies, picking one up from the cabinet.

Mademoiselle stares at us skeptically.

My curiosity is so great that I can't stop myself from asking, "Mademoiselle, forgive me, but I watched you and Rose last night. Did you create a living creature from a root?"

Henri's head pivots sharply toward me, aghast at my boldness.

Ignoring him, I keep my gaze fixed on Mademoiselle as I await her response.

If Henri hadn't also seen the creature, Mademoiselle's incredulous face would make me doubt my own sanity. She looks at me as if I have truly lost my mind. "You must have been dreaming," she says with conviction. "What an idea!"

"I saw it, too." Henri comes to my aid.

"I don't know what you two thought you saw, but there was certainly no living root. We're experimenting with potions that will preserve the quality of the skin until I'm ready to make my masks. Skin hardens so quickly after death that it distorts the likeness."

I don't believe her, but what can I say?

That night when Henri and I creep to our spying place, the rotted wood has been removed and a new wooden patch hammered into place.

$\mathcal{C}$HAPTER 17

It's early in a rainy September that a Revolutionary guardsman comes to the exhibit workroom with a huge bundle slung over his shoulder. It's wrapped in a coarse blanket and heaved without ceremony onto the workroom floor, and the blue-gray foot that peeks out from a fold in the cloth tells me it's a corpse that he's just tossed into the room.

"She was murdered by the citizens of the new Republic of France before she had the honor of being guillotined," the guard tells Mademoiselle Grosholtz, as though this is amusing in some way. "We need two masks. One to parade on a pike so that the people can see what happens to those who would deny the people their rights, and another to keep as a record of French traitors."

Mademoiselle nods listlessly and gestures him toward the door.

"How soon can you have it?" the guard demands without moving.

"I'll send you word," she says, her voice flat as she stares down at the body. With workmanlike detachment, she removes the blanket.

I cry out when I see that the dead body belongs to the Princess de Lamballe, one of Mama's dearest friends. She's hideously slashed, and her entire corpse is marbled with purple-black and yellow bruises.

They've hacked away her luxurious hair, and her face is twisted into an expression of anguished horror.

It's too horrible! I turn away, trembling.

Seeing my distress, Mademoiselle covers the body once again. She takes stationery from a drawer, hastily writes a message, and instructs Henri and me to bring it to Rose at rue du Temple.

"What kind of monsters are these people?" I ask Henri as we walk, heads down against the driving rain.

"We're the ones collecting loose heads," he reminds me.

"But we're forced to."

Henri draws me beside him and puts his arm around my shoulders. "Don't think too much," he advises. "It's easier that way."

I know he's right. I try to push the awful image of the Princess de Lamballe out of my head. Instead, I focus on the warmth of Henri beside me. These days I only feel safe when he's near me, protected from the outside world and also from the demons of fright that run rampant in my mind. These days, if I smile at all, it's only with him.

We find Rose's apartment building and a maid lets us inside. It's a small but elegant place with heavy red velvet drapes, regal furniture, and gold-framed artwork on the walls. Most of the oil paintings depict tropical landscapes, and I wonder if they remind her of her home in Martinique.

Rose sits on a couch in the living room, across from a uniformed military man. His elaborate red jacket lies atop a white shirt, vest, and breeches with tall boots. From his many medals, it's clear he's some sort of general. He's short and has sharp features, and yet he emanates strength and power.

"Perhaps, then, you can speak to Robespierre on behalf of my husband," Rose implores him as she bids us enter with a wave of her hand. "I would so appreciate it, General Bonaparte."

General Bonaparte stands, and bows ceremoniously. "I would do anything you ask of me," he says with feeling. He leans in closer to her. "However, I question the wisdom of your request. It might be better to let the National Assembly forget about you and your husband for now — let sleeping dogs lie, as the saying goes."

Rose rises to her feet. "My husband and I are hardly dogs!"

The general drops to one knee to kiss Rose's hand. "Forgive me, Joséphine."

"Why do you insist on calling me that?" Rose snaps. "My name is Rose."

General Bonaparte stands once more. "Rose is so commonplace. Joséphine suits you better, because you are so rare and beautiful."

He still hasn't noticed us standing in the doorway behind him, and the heat of embarrassment starts to rise in my cheeks. I begin backing out of the room, but Rose raises her hand to stop me.

"Excuse me, General. I have more visitors."

General Bonaparte turns and eyes us with annoyance.

Henri gives Rose the note, and upon reading it she immediately walks General Bonaparte to the door. Then she asks her maid for her cloak. I sneak a peek at the hastily scrawled note: *We have a body at last.*

We trail Rose through the streets, plying her with questions. What are she and Mademoiselle trying to accomplish? Can we help them? If the work is illegal, could they be jailed again?

Rose ignores us as she races through the streets, the hood of her cloak pulled forward.

"Are you using the voodoo you learned when you were a girl in Martinique?" I ask bluntly.

Rose whirls on me, gripping my arm. Her usual smile has disappeared and her tone is uncharacteristically fierce. "You listen, girl," she hisses. "I don't care who or what you are. You are never to speak that word aloud. Ever!"

I've never seen Rose like this.

"I'm sorry," I say, "but why? I only wanted to know if the . . ." I hesitate. "If the . . . island magic is —"

"Forget you ever heard anything about it," Rose commands before resuming her quick path through the streets toward Dr. Curtius's exhibit.

Henri and I exchange a glance, now more intrigued than ever. *What* are they doing?

When we get there, Mademoiselle Grosholtz awaits us by the back door. "I've prepared everything," she says quietly to Rose, as if Henri and I are not there.

"Let us help," Henri pleads. I know he's burning with curiosity as I am.

Mademoiselle ignores him and asks Rose, "Did you bring the potion?"

"I don't know what you mean," Rose says, and her eyes flick to Henri and me.

Mademoiselle Grosholtz takes two rags from a drawer, handing them to Henri and me. "Dr. Curtius wants to reopen the exhibit soon. Every figure must be thoroughly dusted," she instructs. "Rose and I must work on the princess's corpse. We are not to be disturbed."

This is such an obvious ploy to get rid of us that Henri and I just stand there until Mademoiselle erupts, shooing us impatiently out of the workroom.

"We have to find out what they're up to," Henri says when we're in the exhibit.

"It's voodoo for certain," I say. "You saw her reaction when I mentioned it."

Henri nods. "It has to be."

We begin dusting in the ancient Egypt exhibit. I shake the wig Henri has sewn for the Cleopatra figure and dust flies off it. It's been so long since he's dusted the figures that he used to clean twice a week when the exhibit was open.

"Try it on," Henri suggests.

"All right." Using the glass from a framed painting of the pyramids as my mirror, I tuck my short brown hair into the wig. I love the way I look. So exotic.

When I turn to Henri, he's smiling. I blush at the twinkle of admiration in his eyes. "Do you like it?" I ask.

"You look beautiful," he says.

"Beautiful?" I question, pleased. No one's ever called me beautiful before. Mama's always been the beautiful one.

Henri disappears into the ancient Rome room and returns wearing the olive branch wreath, shield, and sword from the Marc Antony figure.

From my studies of both literature and history, I know that Cleopatra and Marc Antony loved each other. With a smile on my face, I leap away from him. "Oh, Marc Antony, you've come all the way from Rome, but I will never fall in love with you. I'm the Queen of the Nile, ruler of all Egypt."

"I will claim you as my queen!" Henri cries. I run across the room away from him, and he chases me. Soon we are racing around the exhibit, me darting away and Henri in pursuit. I hide behind the figure of Pharaoh Akhenaten only to turn and bump right into Henri, who has silently crept up behind.

I cry out in surprise but not for long because Henri covers my mouth in a kiss. At first I'm startled, but then my own emotions swell and I return the kiss with equal fervor.

We kiss and hug each other for what seems like a very long time, there among the famous and infamous figures of the past. I love having Henri in this way, so close and happy.

Finally, Henri takes a deep breath and stands, drawing me to him, holding me firmly with his hand pressed to my back. I allow my head to bend to his shoulder.

"You sound just as royal as Cleopatra ever could have," Henri says. "Do you miss that life very much?"

"Not the life as much as I miss my family."

"Everyone says your family is terrible. They even say it about you," Henri says, still holding me. "But I know you're wonderful, so your family must be wonderful, too."

Pulling back, I look at his adorable face. "I don't know how they've been as rulers," I admit. "I've seen the troubles, and I can't tell how much of it is their fault. I only know that I miss them."

"I'm sure they miss you, too." His voice has become gentle, dreamlike. We begin to rock together, almost as if dancing to some silent music only we can hear. "You're like no one else, Ernestine."

"Say my real name," I whisper in his ear.

He pulls back and looks at me with surprise. Then Henri speaks softly in my ear. "There is no one else like Marie-Thérèse-Charlotte, and I love you more than anyone in this world."

"I love you, too, Henri!" I say, so moved by his words of love. We are kissing once more and I am so very happy. Only with Henri does the awful world disappear. With Henri there's only the two of us and we live on our own island of love where we're safe and nothing else matters.

$\mathcal{C}$HAPTER 18

L ater that night when I awake in my bed, Henri snores lightly on his side of the curtain. The rain has stopped and moonlight brightens the room. I hear voices in the workroom — Mademoiselle and Rose and someone I don't recognize — and slide out of bed.

I want to see who's there, but with the hole in the wall repaired, I can't peer in. So I make my way through the dark exhibit of figures to the front door. I hurry down the dark, puddled street to the back of the exhibit. I lurk by the back window, peering cautiously into the workroom.

I can't hear what they're saying, but what I see astounds me.

The person Mademoiselle Grosholtz and Rose are speaking to is the Princess de Lamballe. Alive!

The women sit around the workshop table with the lamp flickering across their animated faces. The princess speaks from behind her death mask, her face covered, and she waves her arms, describing some horror.

Mademoiselle and Rose are almost comical as they swing from sympathy for the princess — frowning and nodding — to the triumphant elation they share with secretive nods to each other.

Is this the success they've been working toward night after night? Have they truly brought the Princess de Lamballe back to life?

I'm riveted. This is the most bizarre thing I've ever seen!

And then, abruptly, the masked woman slumps forward on the table, arms outstretched.

Mademoiselle and Rose leap up, shaking the woman, gently slapping her cheeks to rouse her. The woman doesn't stir.

Rose slumps into her chair, dejected. Mademoiselle places a comforting hand on Rose's shoulder, but it's clear she feels just as disappointed.

Another failed experiment.

Together they lift the masked woman onto the workshop table. Rose reaches for her cloak, and I know I must leave or risk being discovered as she comes through the door to depart. But what if the corpse rises again? What if it speaks? I don't want to miss any of it.

I linger until Rose is nearly at the door. "I think I know what we need to do. Such a badly injured corpse is too fragile for the shock." As she continues to speak, she begins to open the door, and I flee.

But too late. "Halt!"

Rose hurries toward me, scowling.

"Please don't tell Mademoiselle," I plead. "She'll be so angry with me."

Indecision clouds Rose's beautiful face, and she grabs my arm and begins pulling me along down the street. I have to run to keep up with her forceful stride.

It's late, but a few cafés are still lit and buzzing with activity. She stops at one place alive with people singing around a piano. The crowd here is very well dressed, but they sing revolutionary songs just the same. Maybe it's a way of protecting themselves against the Terror's spies. Perhaps to them, "freedom and liberty" are the fashion of the moment. And, of course, they might be sincere.

When the elegantly dressed host at the door greets Rose as Citizen Beauharnais, she smiles graciously. "I require the general's private room, Citizen Pierre," she says.

The man glances at me skeptically. In my rags I hardly belong in a place like this, but I'm with Rose so he stays silent.

He leads us to a private chamber at the back of the café and leaves us there, shutting the door behind him. It's lovely, with red velvet drapes and furniture. We sit at a highly polished table of deep, gleaming wood. Across the table, Rose studies me for a moment before she speaks. "So, tell me, girl — what did you see?"

"The Princess de Lamballe was back from the dead, wearing the mask of a woman they killed today. The three of you spoke for a while — I heard her voice before I got out of bed. Then she collapsed."

"And what do you make of that?"

"I don't know what to think," I say. "Does it have something to do with what you and Mademoiselle Grosholtz have been working on?"

"You're too smart for your own good," Rose says, more to herself than to me. Then she glances back up at me. "What do you know of the beliefs of ancient Egypt?"

A spark of happiness leaps within me as I tell her the events of the day with Henri, the time spent in the ancient Egypt exhibit. Then I try to recall all I've learned from my royal tutor regarding the Nile and the pyramids, the pharaohs, and ancient gods like Horus and Isis.

"Very good," Rose says. "Do you know why they stored so much wealth in the pyramids?"

"So that the deceased people buried there would have all that they required when their souls returned from the dead."

How does this relate to her experiments? I cannot help but stare expectantly.

Rose sits back in her chair, exasperated. Finally, she slaps the table decisively. "It's better that you don't understand. These things are dark and you're young."

"I don't feel so young," I counter.

"You've seen many things a young woman shouldn't be subjected to," Rose allows. "We're alike in that way. I was about your age when I was sent from Martinique to wed Monsieur de Beauharnais. My older sister had been promised to him, but she passed away."

"My mother was fourteen when she came to Paris," I say. "She was sixteen when she married my father."

"Then she and I have that in common."

"I think she came to love my father," I say, recalling how fond of each other they always are.

"Monsieur de Beauharnais and I have a cordial relationship, though I wouldn't call it love."

"Do you love that general?" I ask.

Rose ponders this a moment before speaking. "I'm not sure. He's interesting to talk to, and he's advancing rapidly within the military. It's helpful to have such an influential suitor."

That might have seemed calculating, but I grew up among the plots and intrigues of the royal court. I know it's simply how the world works.

It was pleasant to sit there talking about love and relationships with Rose. Without Mama or Ernestine, there was no one with which to have this type of girl talk.

"Do you think Mademoiselle Grosholtz has ever been in love?" I ask.

"She has a love," Rose tells me, smiling at my shocked expression. "I believe his name is François Tussaud. He's a civil engineer and is often away, but they correspond regularly."

"I can't imagine Mademoiselle in love," I say, amused and surprised by the idea.

"Everyone loves in their own fashion. Do you love Henri?" Rose asks.

"Yes."

"Don't."

I can't believe what I've heard. "Why not? He's wonderful, and attractive, too. Don't you think so?"

"Listen to me, girl. Things won't always be like this. Even if your family is run out of the country, you will always be a royal. Your family knows you're out here. Sooner or later, they'll send someone to find and reclaim you. You'll be wrenched from Henri and might never see him again. You can't let it break your heart."

"I'll insist that he come with me."

"Don't be naive. They'd never allow it. You must be a friend to him but nothing more. I left a boy behind in Martinique, and I've never forgotten him. I wish I'd never met him rather than to pine for him for the rest of my life."

Pierre comes in to bring us some food, a lobster tail in cream sauce. It is so like something I might have eaten in the palace, and it shocks me that such a delicacy still exists in the world.

We eat in silence, each lost in our own thoughts. I try to imagine life without Henri and find that I can't. We've become so close that he's a part of me.

"You mustn't spy on us anymore," Rose insists after a while. "If you are ever questioned, it could cost you your life."

She won't discuss anything else about the late-night experiments she and Mademoiselle Grosholtz conduct.

Before much longer General Bonaparte appears in the doorway. He beams at Rose, but his smile fades when he notices me. Still, he's polite as he waits for us to finish our meal and then offers us a ride in his carriage. "Get some sleep," Rose advises as I climb out in front of Dr. Curtius's exhibit.

As I settle back into bed, the first glow of dawn is beginning to light the sky. Henri turns on his cot on the other side of the curtain. "Are you okay, Ernestine?" he murmurs.

"Yes, I'm fine," I reply. He turns toward the soft light making its way into the room and I watch him, loving every plane and curve of his face. There can be no future without Henri. I won't allow it.

CHAPTER 19

That winter I read the papers and follow Papa's trial as it's reported. The political cartoons mock Papa unmercifully, depicting him as either a tyrant or a fool. They show Mama dallying with various lords and counts as she spends the country's money frivolously. Why are they so cruel? They don't know my sweet parents at all!

Mademoiselle Grosholtz is sympathetic. She doesn't reprimand me when I wander away from my duties at the foot of the guillotine. Each day I walk the streets, going this way and that, with no particular plan. Or so I tell myself. But I always seem to end up standing outside the Palace du Temple, where they've moved my family, feeling tiny in its monstrous shadow.

Crowds gather outside the ancient, dank palace, hoping to catch a look at the imprisoned royals. I see that some of them carry rotted cabbages to hurl and others wield signs calling for my entire family to die — even little Louis-Charles. Animals! No wonder my family doesn't come out.

A newsboy comes hawking his papers. "Louis Capet stands trial today!"

Louis Capet! The nerve! They won't give Papa the dignity of his proper title. Capet isn't even his name, but refers to a branch of the Bourbon family. Idiots!

A man buys a paper, peruses the headlines, and then tosses it in the trash. Despite my growing hatred of these papers, the desire to know what's going on with Papa overpowers me. I quickly fish it out and read the story.

The news couldn't be worse. There's a quote from a revolutionary named Danton calling for the execution of my entire family. In the past, Danton has been considered moderate in his views. If one such as he is against us, what hope can there be?

"You know how to read?" I look up at a man standing watching me.

"No, Citizen," I lie quickly. "I'm looking at the drawings."

He takes the paper from me. "Ah, yes," he comments. "They're finally getting around to killing the king. It's about time."

"I don't see why they don't simply exile him," I say. "Why does he have to die?"

"Because he'd just come back with an Austrian army and retake the country. And where would the French people be then?"

"I don't know," I say. "Where *would* they be?"

"Right back where we started from, that's where — with the royals sucking up whatever's left of the nation's wealth with their lavish ways while the rest of us starve!"

"What if they changed that, stopped living so well?"

The man laughs uproariously. "Small chance of that happening! Those selfish monsters! Believe me, Citizen, you'll be much better off when freedom and liberty ring across this country, and it won't happen until every last one of the royals is beheaded."

"Even the little boy?" I challenge, the blood rising in my cheeks. "He's only a child, you know."

"Even him," the man insists. "Little boys grow up to be men who carry grudges. What's to stop him from rallying foreign kings to help him? They'd be glad to. They must all be scared for their own necks right about now. The sacred truth of liberty is spreading. The fire of freedom has been lit. Better days are coming, Citizen. Mark my words." He nods toward the paper. "Mind if I keep this?"

"No, go ahead," I reply.

Henri appears. He knows by now where to find me. "We're done," he says.

I nod, still looking at the Temple prison.

"Why do you torture yourself?" he asks.

"I'm trying to figure out how to get inside."

Henri sighs deeply and grabs my hand. "Come on. Mademoiselle wants you to come right away. She has work for us."

On the way back, I suddenly stop, gripping Henri's arm. "Look, there!" I say, pointing. A man in a toga strolls across the street. His hair is thinning and he wears a crown of olive leaves.

It's Julius Caesar, just as he appears in the exhibit.

It's a cold December day and the man's thin toga flaps around his knobby knees, but he seems not to notice. With an upswept arm, he shields his face from the blustery wind and turns in a circle as though he's lost.

"It can't be," Henri murmurs.

I'm so glad Henri is with me, or I'd think I'm going mad.

"Perhaps he's come from a costume party or a play," I say. I hurry forward to address him. "Excuse me, Citizen, can I direct you somewhere?"

"The river?" he asks.

"The Seine is that way," I tell him, pointing.

Henri steps forward. "We can walk with you if you'd —" He doesn't even get to finish his sentence before Julius Caesar rushes past him in the direction of the Seine at the center of Paris.

Henri and I shift on our feet, not sure if we should pursue him or not. "Mademoiselle will be angry if we don't come back," Henri says.

Nodding in agreement, I fall into step with Henri and return to the exhibit. It's quiet with no one else around, and Henri and I enter the ancient Rome exhibit. I gasp at what I see — or rather, don't see.

The wax figure of Julius Caesar is gone!

Mademoiselle Grosholtz enters and there's an expression of panic on her face. It seems the figure's disappearance is also a shock to her. She tries to conceal her anxiety by turning away from us.

"What happened to the Roman emperor?" Henri asks.

When Mademoiselle Grosholtz turns back toward us, her face is once again set in the emotionless visage of neutrality so common to her. "Dr. Curtius is working on it at the other exhibit," she says. "It's in need of repair."

"It couldn't be alive and walking the streets of Paris, could it?" Henri dares to suggest.

"You saw him?!" she cries, dropping her mask of calm.

"He was walking out on the street just now," I confirm.

"Where? Tell me!"

"Rue de Gare," Henri says. "He was headed toward the Seine."

Mademoiselle Grosholtz plucks her cloak off the hook by the front door and throws it around her shoulders. "I'll be right back."

"Has the figure come to life?" I ask.

"I'm afraid that's quite impossible," Mademoiselle Grosholtz says as she hurries toward the front door. "These figures are nothing but wax and wire. What a ridiculous thing to say!"

"But then what —" My words are cut off by the slamming of the front door as Mademoiselle goes out.

"Should we follow?" I ask Henri.

With a nod, Henri heads for the door after her, and I'm right behind. We trail her to rue de Gare and keep on toward the river.

At the stone wall bordering the Seine — where they sell newspapers, paintings, and all sorts of trinkets — Mademoiselle Grosholtz peers down at the river that flows through Paris. Seeming to find what she's searching for, she heads down the steps toward the water.

"She might see us if we follow her down there," I point out to Henri as we rush to the wall.

"Look!" Henri says.

Mademoiselle Grosholtz sits on a bench by the river and beside her is Julius Caesar. Her arm is around his shoulders, and Mademoiselle seems to be comforting him as he sobs into his hands.

Henri and I exchange a look of utter bewilderment.

After a while they get up and head for the stairs leading back to the street. I follow Henri as he scrambles behind a newspaper stand by the wall, crouching low so as not to be seen when Mademoiselle comes up with her companion.

Arm in arm, they walk through the street. Mademoiselle pays no attention to the perplexed and amused glances she and Julius Caesar are attracting. She is very tender with her strange friend, leaning in attentively as he speaks softly, his head down.

We follow them until they arrive at Rose's apartment on rue du Temple, not far from where my family is imprisoned. They enter together.

"Maybe he's a lunatic from the asylum," Henri speculates.

"Could he have stolen the Caesar costume from the exhibit?"

Henri shrugs. "Come on," he says. "I know a shortcut back to the exhibit. We'll get there before she ever knows we were gone."

We turn in the opposite direction, about to cut across the street, but our path is blocked as a tumbrel full of prisoners turns the corner. How I hate these carts that take the prisoners to the guillotine!

"It's the girl and boy who collect the heads!" a woman on the cart shouts, pointing at us.

The woman beside her twists her face grotesquely and crosses her eyes. "How do you like my head?" she calls. "I'll be sure to stick my tongue out for you before they drop the blade." The two women keep up the jeers, adding rude gestures until the tumbrel pulls out of sight.

I stand there, ashamed of what we do and embarrassed.

"Would you rather that Mademoiselle goes to the guillotine?" Henri asks, reading the discomfort on my face.

"No," I say. Despite Mademoiselle's standoffish ways, she's been good to me, and I've grown to respect her talent and appreciate her kindness.

"Then it's what has to be done," Henri assures me. "The people are dead. We're not the ones who've killed them."

Henri is always able to make me feel better. Holding hands, we head back toward the exhibit, moving through the web of back alleys Henri knows so well.

CHAPTER 20

There's not much celebration on my birthday, but Henri takes me to the woman who makes powdered sugar crêpes on the corner and buys me one of them drizzled in chocolate. It's wonderful, and makes me think how foolish I was to once take treats such as these for granted.

"I'm sure your birthday would be a lot grander if you were home," he says.

I give him a bite of my crêpe. He only had money for one. "This is the best birthday present I've ever received," I assure him. Maybe that's not exactly true, but I haven't had a dessert treat in so long. Henri must have saved for it for many weeks, and that means a lot to me.

Henri smiles at me. "I'm glad you like it. This woman is the best crêpe maker in all Paris. At least I think so." Turning, I look back at her, so ragged, standing there by her big homemade griddle. She was thrilled when we asked for a crêpe, and now she has no other customers.

We return to the exhibit, and inside we're amazed to see Julius Caesar has returned to the ancient Rome exhibit, once more inanimate and made of wax. To be honest, he looks a bit worse for wear, stooped but with a wild-eyed expression. Somehow he appears to be more human than before he disappeared. I poke him, just to be sure. His smooth waxiness comes off on my fingers.

It feels as though seeing him alive was a dream.

"He was real," Henri says, reading my mind. "We both saw him."

"I know," I agree with a nod. The world has become so grotesque, it seems to me that almost anything can be real. What is the difference between having one's head cut off for no reason other than not wearing a tricolored ribbon and having a wax figure of Julius Caesar come to life and then return to its original state? Which reality is more bizarre? I think it's pretty hard to say.

"Cleopatra's gone now," Henri notices. And sure enough, she is.

Mademoiselle Grosholtz comes in, and I see how tired she seems. She notices us staring at the place where Cleopatra once stood. "It's being cleaned," she says.

I meet her gaze and my expression is full of skepticism. She has to know we don't believe her.

"Dr. Curtius is also making repairs," she adds as she moves on into the workroom.

"She goes out at night lately," Henri tells me when she's gone.

"Maybe her suitor is in town," I suggest, "Monsieur Tussaud."

"If that's so, he must live in a mudhole. I saw the clothing she piled up to be laundered. It's filthy, caked in dirt."

"Really?"

"Yes. And look at her hands. They've suddenly become cal-loused." Mademoiselle's hands have always seemed nearly porcelain to me, smooth and delicate. What can she be doing?

It is early on a dark, gray January morning when I come in upon Mademoiselle Grosholtz and Rose talking. Henri smiles up at me as he files the rough edges from the wax face of a soldier who'd been beheaded yesterday afternoon.

"We have to work very fast now," Mademoiselle says to Rose. Their backs are to me and they don't know I'm there. "Just this after-noon, the National Convention reversed their original decision and voted to behead the king."

To behead the king.

To behead . . .

Her words ring through my mind. My blood is ice, my brain fro-zen. It will not allow this information in.

I stand, stupefied. There's a screaming inside me but it's still very far away.

"Ernestine!" Henri cries out, putting down his work and hurrying to my side.

Rose gasps as she turns toward me. "I'm so sorry! I didn't know you were there!"

The room is spinning. I slide to the floor.

There are great black openings in the universe that swirl around my head, cavernous mouths threatening to engulf me, and then one succeeds, sucking me into its blackness. I am floating there beyond the reach of light or sound or hunger or pain — untouchable, safe from the world, a hideous world where words can slice like razor blades with words like . . .

. . . *voted to behead the king.*

Papa! Oh, my sweet, dear Papa! It can't be true. It can't be.

I come back to consciousness as Henri lifts me into his arms. I lean heavily on him while he guides me back to the bedroom. I'm too numb to even speak, but he sits beside me in my bed and strokes my hair. Once he kisses me on the top of my head, I start to cry, burying my face in his chest.

"They're going to kill my father, Henri," I say softly. Will we carry his head home in a basket? How can I bear it?

I'm now more determined than ever to get into the prison to see Papa. My plan is to dress as a royal and let myself be captured sneaking out. The guards will throw me back inside the prison, and then I'll be with my family.

To this end I borrow a dress from myself. At least, from the wax figure of me from the dismantled dinner exhibit in the wax museum's basement. When the frenzied crowd grabbed the heads of my parents to parade around on spikes, Dr. Curtius decided that the exhibit was putting the entire museum at risk. He took it down, but the figures of Louis-Charles and me are still intact.

Struggling into the dress my wax figure wears reveals how much I've grown in this time. It's much too tight, so I take pieces from other discarded figures, like Madame de Pompadour's bodice, and a shawl from Anne Boleyn. I take a blonde wig from a wax figure I can't identify.

Dressed like this, I hurry to the front door while Mademoiselle and Henri are in the workroom. Before going out, I hesitate, realizing I may never see either of them again. I hurry back into the bedroom and quickly write Henri a note on the blank back of an advertising card someone handed me in the street.

Henri, I must go to my papa. If I don't come back, know that I will never forget you. You are forever in my heart.

I know he can't read it, but someone will do that for him. I couldn't stand to go away without leaving even a word for him.

Would I be heartbroken if Henri ran out on me like I'm doing to him? Yes.

Do I have any choice? No.

If I tell him what I intend to do, he will surely stop me, using whatever means possible.

CHAPTER 21

*I*t's very cold, and I shiver in my thin shawl. As I loiter near the gate of the Palace du Temple, I peer in at the guards hoping they'll notice me soon.

I'm about to give up hope when a horse-drawn cart approaches. The driver calls to be let in. As the guard approaches, I scramble around back and climb up, hiding under the canvas-covered food supplies being delivered.

The gates clank and squeal as the guard draws them back.

In minutes I'm rocked by the cart moving forward.

I'm inside!

The moment the cart stops, I intend to come out and run for the door, but the tarp over the food is abruptly yanked off. "Trying to escape, are you?" the guard shouts at me. "How did you get out here?"

Easier than I expected. I look at him wide-eyed but don't speak, only cower. And this fear is not entirely put on. There is no amusement in his expression. He's red-faced yet triumphant in his discovery of me. I'm his captive, and even though I've deliberately thrown myself into his path, my captivity suddenly scares me. What have I done?

The guard grips my arm with painful force as he yanks me out of the cart.

"You're hurting me!" I cry.

"You should have thought of that before you tried to escape," the guard snaps, bustling me into the palace. I cough in the dank, closed air of the interior, barely warmer than that outside.

The change from what I remember of the place is immense. There is not a painting on the wall, nor a piece of furniture anywhere — not a rug, nor a chandelier, not even curtains on the windows. The shuttered windows add greatly to the feeling of gloom within. The stones emanate cold.

"This way, *Citizen*," the guard barks, yanking my arm roughly. He moves so quickly that he's almost dragging me as he hurries down a long shadowy hall and then up a winding staircase. Another hallway takes us to a tower.

Although it was cold in the palace, this tower is almost as frigid as being outdoors. The shuttered windows are narrow, allowing in the barest shards of light. I tremble as I gaze at my surroundings. The thought of being trapped here is awful, much worse than I have ever imagined it would be.

The guard opens a door and shoves me inside. "Keep a better eye on your daughter," he shouts as my family looks at him, stunned. "None of you will eat today to remind you to cooperate."

He slams the door behind him as he leaves, and we hear the bolt clank.

Everyone stares in disbelief, but my family's faces are the only ones I can see: Papa, Mama, Louis-Charles, and Ernestine. In his outrage, the guard didn't even notice that there were two Princess Marie-Thérèse-Charlottes!

Thank goodness!

Mama is the first to speak. "Marie-Thérèse! What have you done?"

"And how?" Papa adds.

Ernestine wraps me in a hug. "I've missed you beyond words. We all have!"

I've missed them, too, and maybe I haven't realized how much until this moment. In the next minutes they all gather round, embracing me. Everyone is crying, except Louis-Charles, who is all smiles.

When we calm down, Mama is full of questions. She wants to know where I'm living, whether I have enough to eat, and if I am being treated well. I assure her I'm fine. "Then why have you come here?" she asks.

"I had to see . . . all of you." I can't bring myself to say I wanted to see my father one more time before his death. It's just too painful.

And suddenly it strikes me — do they even know he's been condemned to die?

Papa extends his arms, and I walk into them as he folds me in a hug. Pressing my head to his chest, I hear his heartbeat — his good, big heart!

As the evening progresses, I realize that they don't know what Papa's fate will be. They talk about what they'll do when the current situation is over. Looking forward to the future is what keeps them strong. To tell them what I know would only bring them pain.

"You know I'm going to have to hide now," Ernestine says. "We got lucky tonight, but every guard is not as oblivious to who is actually in here."

"I'm sorry," I apologize.

Ernestine nods. "It's all right. We're together again and that's what matters."

Papa and Mama each have separate chambers. Monsieur Cléry sleeps with Papa. Madame de Tourzel shares another room with Aunt Élisabeth. Louis-Charles sleeps in a room with me and Ernestine. He quickly falls asleep on his narrow divan, but Ernestine and I are too excited to sleep. We lie together on the large bed speaking in confiding whispers, just like old times. It's wonderful.

We talk quietly into the night. I tell her all about Henri and how I adore him. "He sounds wonderful," Ernestine says. "It's too bad that you're engaged to Louis-Antoine."

"I can't possibly marry the duc de Angouleme now that I've found Henri. And if they do away with the monarchy, maybe I won't have to."

"But he's so nice!" Ernestine protests.

"You liked him even more than I did."

"Oh, we got on so well," Ernestine recalls. "I'll tell you a secret: That night after he visited, I was jealous of you, that you'd get to marry him."

It all seems too far in the future to think about — and too distant in the past to remember. "Who knows what the future holds?" I say.

"That's true," Ernestine agrees. "Tell me more about life outside here."

She gasps when I unpin my blonde wig and reveal my short brown hair. "This is the new me," I say with a grin.

Ernestine runs her hand along my head in wonder. "You look so different," she remarks. "It's not very fashionable, is it?"

"No," I agree, ruffling out my real hair, "but it's so light and easy to keep. I've grown to like it."

I tell her about the strange experiments that go on at night. I talk about the walking ginger root, but I don't say anything about the Princess de Lamballe. Ernestine knew her well and might not even know of her brutal death. I decide it would be too upsetting to mention.

Ernestine's intrigued when I recount the conversation I had with Rose. "Ancient Egypt was such a mysterious place," she remarks. "It's so odd the way they buried royal figures with all their things so they could come back to use them in the next life. They must have really believed it was possible, for them to go to all that trouble."

"But why do you suppose Rose mentioned that? What was she trying to tell me?"

Ernestine leans close and whispers, "I think they're using Rose's magic to bring the wax figures to life — don't you think so? The moving root was only an experiment."

Of course!

That's what it has to be!

But it's such an outrageous idea that I can't be too upset that it didn't occur to me. "Do you really think so?"

"She admits she was trained in mystical arts, doesn't she?"

"Rose learned from a priestess who knew about spells using herbs and roots and all that kind of thing."

Ernestine nods knowingly. "That's why she brought up ancient Egypt. It's all a version of the same thing. They're moving the spirits of the dead into the wax figures — or at least they're trying to. They're bringing them back from the guillotine!"

Ernestine and I stare at each other, awestruck by the audacity of the idea.

"That's it!" Ernestine insists confidently.

Although Ernestine and I eventually settle down to sleep, I can't quiet my mind. There's nothing but wax and wire inside these figures. How could they stay alive?

Then I think of the Princess de Lamballe.

Is that why Mademoiselle and Rose were so excited when the princess's body was delivered to them? Is it why the princess wore the mask of another that night when she seemed to come alive? Ernestine was only partly right.

What if the wax figures can only hold a spirit for a brief period of time before they have to be transferred into a real flesh body?

The thought gives me chills, and I sit upright in the bed, wrapping my arms around my knees. There in the dark, I'm very afraid. These are elemental forces of life and death that Rose and Mademoiselle are toying with. They are crossing the line between the two.

But why are they doing this? Who are they bringing back from the dead?

CHAPTER 22

The days pass with excruciating boredom. The guards refuse to give us paper or new books. There isn't even an open window to look out of. Ernestine and I tell Louis-Charles every story we can remember and even make up some new ones. But the constant talking becomes exhausting, and we often fall into a dull lethargy.

The only excitement comes when one of us — either Ernestine or I — must hide from a guard or a servant delivering food. We decide to take turns hiding so no one forms a clear picture of what I look like. No matter which one of us is called into question, someone will confirm that it is indeed Marie-Thérèse-Charlotte who is being presented.

We have one luxury that we share — each of us is granted a brief, daily walk in the Temple Garden. I go one day, and Ernestine goes the next. Crowds amass at the high, spiked iron gate and shout rude, obscene things at us, so I try to stay toward the back of the garden when it's my turn to walk.

One day, while toward the back of the gardens, I find a chink in the high stone wall. Through it I can see a pleasant little park area with only a few people sitting, talking, or reading. I like to look through it, pretending my life is that serene.

I tell Ernestine about the spot and the lovely view and she delights in it as well. We make up a new game: What did you see through the chink in the wall? Each reports what she saw that day — a spotted spaniel, children running, an unusual bird. It gives us something fun to do in the evening.

The days move so slowly, and not a moment passes when I don't think about Henri. Is he well? What is he doing? Does he hate me for running out or does he understand?

I try to spend as many afternoons as I can with Papa. When I was a girl, he spoiled me with beautiful toys, clothing, and books, and also with his time. He walked with me in the gardens and showed me how to work the locks that he loved to build and fix.

One day, I knock at his chamber door and find him at a splintered desk, tinkering with the insides of a clock. "Come in, sweet girl," he invites me. "How are you holding up under these miserable conditions?"

Sitting on the edge of his desk, I shrug and pick up a gear, turning it in my hands. "I'm happy to be back with everyone, though I miss the friends I've made in Paris."

"You have friends in Paris, eh?" he says, smiling forlornly. "Unfortunately, I can't say the same."

I want to insist that he still has supporters, that there are those who remain loyal. But those loyalists have been terrorized into silence or have fled for fear of their lives.

"Pull that chair over, Marie-Thérèse," Papa says. "I must talk to you about something important."

My heart races with anxiety. What is he about to say?

When I am seated beside him, he takes my hands in his. "My girl, you've already been through more than a young woman should have to bear, but I fear that another terrible blow will be ahead for you. It seems there has been a vote —"

Standing, I throw myself into his side, my face instantly soaked in tears. "I know, Papa! It's too awful, but I've known for two weeks." What can I say? There's nothing! All I can do is sob, racked by my own helpless grief.

Papa hugs me to him, saying nothing but just letting me cry. After a while, when the intensity of my sobbing subsides, he brushes back a lock of damp hair that's fallen into my face. "Listen to me, Marie-Thérèse-Charlotte, we cannot change what can't be changed. I go to my death with the conviction that I've done all I can to compromise with the revolutionaries. Perhaps a smarter man than I could have figured a way around all this madness, but I've done what I can do. In the future, I want you to know that I've loved you and our family with all my heart, and you have been my greatest source of joy in this life."

I cry out as his words tear my heart apart. Once more I sob into his shoulder. This time, he won't have it. "Stop, my girl. You have to be strong, now more than ever. Your mother will depend on you, and so will Louis-Charles. If you ever see an opportunity to get out of here, take it. You can work for us better if you're free." He looks me over and his face softens. "But I am so happy to see you again before . . ." He hesitates and then hugs me to him. "Before my time comes."

On January 21, the guards come for Papa. He'd said good-bye to all of us the night before, amidst much weeping. This is breaking my heart! He's the sweetest Papa in the world. It can't be really happening, though I know it is.

With the windows shuttered we can't see his tumbrel clatter away, but we hear the drums that accompany Papa's departure from the Temple prison.

Several hours later, we all sit listlessly, draped despondently around the room. The door opens and a guard appears with our meals. With him is a woman I recognize because I've seen her in the public squares of Paris speaking against my family with the Society of Revolutionary Republican Women. Her name is Claire Lacombe, but she's called Red Rosa. Her appearance here frightens me. What could she want with us?

"I am taking the princess," Red Rosa announces harshly.

Aunt Élisabeth rises from her chair, but Red Rosa waves her away. "The young princess," Red Rosa says.

Ernestine has stepped behind a curtain, and I stand in front of her. Which of us should go? Who would be better off?

Mama steps toward Red Rosa. "What do you want with my daughter?" she asks boldly.

Red Rosa swings around and locks the door. We watch her in amazement.

Mama stands in front to shield me. "You leave her alone," she cries.

Ernestine steps out from behind the curtain, emboldened by her desire to protect me.

"Your Highness, I'm a friend," Red Rosa says. "These are but disguises crafted by Mademoiselle Grosholtz."

I know her voice now. "Rose?" I ask.

"Yes, yes, it's me."

"And me," the guard finally speaks.

"Henri!" I whisper, shocked. Their masks are so lifelike, but now I realize it's wax that's adhered to their faces and has been molded into the likeness of Red Rosa and into the image of one of the guards.

"For weeks now I've been forging letters to the revolutionaries, claiming to be Red Rosa, saying I want to take the princess to my society and make her admit her crimes against the people of France," Rose explains.

"She has no crimes to admit," Mama says.

"No," Rose tells her. "It's just an excuse."

"This is Rose and Henri, the ones I've been telling you about," I say. "They're my friends. You can trust them."

"Hurry, then," Mama says.

"Be sure to keep Ernestine out of sight until midnight tonight," Rose instructs Mama.

"My Mousseline Serieuse," Mama coos as she holds me tight. "My brave girl." A tear rolls down my cheek at her words.

Still misty-eyed, I hug everyone. Louis-Charles clings to my neck so tightly that Mama must gently pull him off. "Until we meet again," I say.

Ernestine squeezes my hand, and with a last wave, I follow Rose and Henri out the door. Our descent down the winding stairs and through the dim, dank corridors to the front courtyard of the Temple seems to take forever. At every moment, I'm sure someone will appear to challenge us. But eventually we emerge into the day-light outside.

I squint into the sunlight.

Rose and Henri pull me into an alley, where Rose quickly takes the pins from my blonde wig and ruffles my hair. "We don't want this crowd thinking you are who you are," she explains.

In the weeks I've been imprisoned, the blonde roots of my hair have grown back. "Here, put this on," Rose says, pulling one of the revolutionary red caps from the bag she carries beneath her cloak.

The next thing she does is to peel the wax from her face. It comes off in chunks. "Thank goodness Mademoiselle Grosholtz reminded me to oil my skin before I put this on," she says as her own skin emerges, blotched red from the wax.

Henri also peels off his wax mask. When he's done, I fall into his arms, and he kisses me.

"Young love is grand, but not now," Rose chides us mildly. "Let's get off the street as quickly as possible."

The three of us keep our heads down as we stride purposefully along the boulevards. All around us there is celebration: people — some of them already drunk — wheeling around the streets, singing and cheering. "Is it a holiday?" I ask Henri.

He doesn't answer and his expression is pale. Why doesn't he answer me?

And then I realize why.

They're celebrating the death of the king.

"The king is dead. Long live the Republic!" someone in the crowd shouts.

Tears jump to my eyes. Henri pulls me to him, enfolding me in his arms. "Don't let them see you cry," he whispers sharply. I know we could be sentenced to death for even such a mild show of disloyalty to the Republic as that, so I dash away the wetness from my cheeks.

"It's Henri and Ernestine, the head collectors!" a woman shouts.

All eyes turn toward us. "Where's the king's head?" a man asks us. "Do you have it? Let's see!"

"They don't have it," Rose intervenes. "It's being worked on."

"They've got it," the man insists. "Give it to us."

The man is in the lead as a crowd begins to circle us. I grip Henri's hand tightly. I've seen all too many times what one of these mobs will do to someone who makes it unhappy.

Rose steps in front of us, holding up the letter to Claire Lacomb, which bears the seal of the National Assembly on the top. "We are citizens employed in the people's business," she tells them in a fierce, commanding tone. "Anyone who interferes with us will find themselves on the scaffold at the Place de la Révolution."

The crowd disperses almost immediately, and Rose hurries us onward until we're at the back door of the workroom. Mademoiselle Grosholtz is there, pacing anxiously. "Thank God!" she cries when we appear, but this is the last she speaks of my having been gone for weeks. Instead, she's all about the business at hand.

"I don't know if we've already waited too long," she says to Rose.

"Perhaps not, though," Rose replies, throwing off her cape.

They hurry to the worktable, where a figure lies in a supine position. It's draped with a sheet.

When Rose yanks off the sheet, I stagger back into Henri.

The figure on the table is Papa!

I run to him and then recoil. He's wax — only a wax image of my father. With questioning eyes, I look at Rose and Mademoiselle. What is this? What's going on?

"This is the event we've been working toward for so long," Rose says. "We want to capture your father's spirit, but we must know his real name. What is it?"

"Louis the Sixteenth of France, of course," I say, too stunned to question further. "King Louis the Sixteenth."

"No," Mademoiselle Grosholtz protests. "We need his real name in order to call to your father's authentic spirit. What's his given name?"

I stare at her blankly. "I don't know it."

"Is it Louis Capet?" Rose presses.

I shake my head, knowing that this is something the revolutionaries call him, but they're wrong. Papa told me that his family isn't descended from the Capetian dynasty as the people think.

"Is it Louis Bourbon?" Mademoiselle suggests.

"Yes, that might be it," I say, not sure, but knowing Bourbon is a family name.

"That will have to do," Rose decides. "Time is running out." She puts Henri and me to work with all sorts of tasks. We sprinkle the life-size wax figure with foul-smelling powders and dab it with rose water. We draw the curtains at the back window and position lit white candles around the room.

Along with the large figure of Papa, Mademoiselle has created a twelve-inch wax figurine of him, which Rose wraps in a soft cloth and holds just far enough above a candle flame that it doesn't melt.

"Louis Bourbon, King of France," Rose intones as she holds the figure with one hand and passes her other hand back and forth over it. "We call your spirit to this place. We call your spirit to this place. We call your spirit to this place."

The fingers on Papa's life-size image twitch.

We all stare, awestruck.

"Louis Bourbon, keep coming to us. We are here to welcome you. Your daughter, Marie-Thérèse-Charlotte, is here. She doesn't want your spirit to leave this earthly plane. We can help you," Rose continues, speaking with fervent passion. She turns to me. "Call your father! Guide him here!"

"Come back, Papa!" I cry out, letting go of any doubt I felt about this. "It's me, Marie-Thérèse! Come to me."

Abruptly, the figure grips my wrist and I scream.

"No! No!" Mademoiselle says to me. "Be loving. Call to him."

Tears now stream down my cheeks. "Come, Papa! Please! Please! Don't leave me. I'm out here all alone. I'm alone. Don't leave me!"

Then I hear Papa's voice. But it's not coming from the figure. It's in the air — a disembodied voice.

"Marie-Thérèse! Don't cry, my dear girl."

It's Papa!

"I can't stay. I have to move on. They're calling me now."

"Papa!" I shout, desperate. "Stay! Don't go!"

"I love you, Marie-Thérèse-Charlotte. Don't forget me."

The hand loosens its grip and falls away from my wrist.

"Papa!" I cry out.

Sobs rack my body and I fall onto the floor in a heap.

I'm consumed with sorrow. I am sorrow. There is nothing left to me.

Henri kneels beside me, rubbing his hand up and down my heaving spine. "You're not alone, Marie-Thérèse," he soothes. "I'm here. You'll never be alone."

$\mathcal{C}$HAPTER 23

*I*n the next months, I'm grateful for all the activity because it takes my mind off worrying about my family. Rose takes me into her confidence and shows me her book collection about the mystic powers of voodoo.

In these books, which are yellowed and cracked and handwritten, I read about the energies of the universe, and how they can be harnessed.

It seems like magic to me, but Rose assures me that it isn't. "The spirit world, like the living world, is composed of energetic forces that work in ways we don't understand," she says. "But the more information one has about these elemental forces, the better we are able to control and direct them. These things were once known in Africa, both by the tribal peoples and the ancient Egyptians, but as the old Egyptian culture declined and the Africans were spread across the planet, the knowledge has been lost."

"But not lost, because it's preserved in these books," I point out.

Rose opens the book to the inside back cover, and I can see that a chunk of the last pages have been torn out. "Perhaps these papers exist somewhere to this day," she says, "but they're not here. That's why I've been trying to approximate the words of the spells and the ingredients of the potions."

I nod, thinking of how it seems she almost captured Papa's spirit within the wax figure Mademoiselle made of him, but then failed.

"So how does it work? How does the spirit know where to go?"

"We have to find a way to direct the spirit to the wax figure," Rose replies, "and then we have to find a vessel for it to live within that can allow it to survive."

"Do you mean a real body?"

Rose nods solemnly. "The body has to be found within hours of its death, before decay sets in."

I wonder what it would be like to suddenly find myself in another body. I don't think I'd like that, though I suppose it would depend on how like my own body the replacement was. A girl my own age might be all right. But what if I landed inside the body of a hairy butcher, or an old woman? I shudder at the idea.

Would I still be me? Would I be part me and part them?

I'm helping Mademoiselle spread warm wax on the oiled face of Charlotte Corday, who killed the Terror leader Marat, when there's a thumping at the back door. Mademoiselle Grosholtz sighs with irritation. She doesn't like being disturbed when she's creating a mask.

"See who it is, would you?" she requests of me. "Check at the window before you open the door."

Gently, I part the curtain of the back window and see a woman in her twenties. She would be beautiful if her face wasn't battered, swollen with purple bruises. "Mademoiselle, it's a woman. She's hurt," I reply.

Mademoiselle leaves her work and is quickly at my side looking out the window. She gasps at the sight, hurrying to let the woman in.

The woman collapses into her arms. "Brigitte, who did this to you?" Mademoiselle demands to know, outraged.

Brigitte? She does look familiar, now that I look past the bruises. I've seen her before but I can't remember where.

"I've been accused of spying for the duc d'Orléans," Brigitte says in a halting, faint voice. "I ran from the guards who came to arrest me, but a crowd formed and chased me."

"They did this to you?" Mademoiselle asks.

Brigitte nods.

Henri comes in from the other doorway where he's been listening. He swears softly when he sees the condition Brigitte is in. "How did you get away?" he asks.

"They thought I was dead and left me in the street," Brigitte tells us.

Mademoiselle instructs me to get cool water and a soft cloth. She sends Henri for bandages. Together, Mademoiselle and Henri walk Brigitte to my bed and lay her down gently. "Go to Rose's apartment and tell her I need some of her herbal remedies," Mademoiselle says with quiet urgency.

"I've seen that woman somewhere before," I say to Henri as we head out for Rose's apartment.

"Of course you have," Henri replies. "We were together the last time I saw her. Think, you'll remember."

"The Belle Zulima!" I cry. I recall my shock when her large blue eyes unexpectedly snapped open and then winked at me. Her delicate features are so swollen now, her silken hair soaked in blood.

"Do you think she'll live?" I ask Henri.

"I don't know," he admits, and we begin to run toward Rose's apartment.

CHAPTER 24

With the help of Mademoiselle's care and Rose's remedies, Brigitte does not die. But she's hardly alive. She lies in my bed drifting in and out of sleep. It becomes my duty to make sure she eats the herb-infused vegetable broth Rose's maid brings every day. I sit on the edge of my former bed, spooning it into Brigitte's mouth, wiping the drips with a cloth.

At night I sleep on a straw-stuffed mattress beside Brigitte and have the same dream of her lying in her glass case. Again and again I relive the moment her eyes opened and she gave me that mischievous wink. In the dream, though, I'm not frightened. This time I understand that the wink means we are partners in something, some plan.

As Brigitte improves ever so slowly, we sometimes stay awake whispering at night.

Brigitte tells me how her great, astonishing beauty has been a blessing but also a curse. "Men see only that," she says. "It's hard to know if a man loves me for myself or only loves my beauty."

"I never thought of that," I say.

"How can that be? You're a beautiful girl."

"I don't have much experience in love," I admit. "Though there is someone."

In the morning, I awake to find that Henri is not in his bed. Dressing quickly, I find him in the workroom already laying out the tools for the day's work.

When I enter the room, he looks up at me and smiles. I come beside him and he clasps my hand. "I heard you talking last night," he says softly.

"You did?"

"I want you to know something," he says. "It's important."

"What?" I ask.

"I love the beauty that you show on the outside. But it's your lovely inner person that I adore."

Pulling away slightly, I study his face. He's not making fun or being flippant. He is completely sincere.

The immensity of my love for Henri overpowers me, and I kiss him hard on the lips. He returns the kiss with full passion. Our love is so strong that I know nothing can ever come between us.

One day in July, Mademoiselle's mysterious suitor, François Tussaud, appears at the workshop. Mademoiselle is completely transformed, no longer the severe, serious person we are used to but a smiling, radiant woman.

Monsieur Tussaud seems pleasant, if shy, as he embraces her in the workroom. I'm sanding the rough bumps from Charlotte Corday's death mask, making her skin lustrous, in the corner of the room while Henri sweeps. Mademoiselle Grosholtz and Monsieur Tussaud talk as though they've forgotten we're here.

"It's no longer safe for us in France," he tells her. "We both have ties to the old regime. The revolutionaries see everything as a sign of loyalty to the monarchy."

"But neither of us has aided the royals," Mademoiselle points out.

"It doesn't matter. It's all madness. No one is safe. Anna Marie, marry me and we'll go to London."

Monsieur Tussaud's proposal shocks Mademoiselle, I can tell by her expression, and she's speechless.

"Come away with me," Monsieur Tussaud presses softly.

"I can't, at least, not right now," Mademoiselle Grosholtz answers tenderly, reaching out to stroke his hair. "If I leave, the National Assembly will come after Dr. Curtius, maybe even Mother. They might take revenge on them."

"But you would come if it were possible?" Monsieur Tussaud wants to be assured.

"Absolutely," Mademoiselle says. "I would love to marry you. As soon as this insanity passes, we'll go."

Henri and I exchange worried glances. Mademoiselle Grosholtz has been our benefactor, our protector, our friend. What would our lives be like without her?

Henri comes alongside me, still sweeping. "We'll go with her," he says quietly.

I suddenly understand how Mademoiselle Grosholtz feels. How can I go with my family still imprisoned? But I hold my tongue. What's the point? Who knows what the future holds?

Then Monsieur Tussaud says something that makes my blood run cold.

"The queen and the dauphin, Louis-Charles, have been separated from the others."

"Where have they been taken?" I blurt.

He pauses for a moment. "The queen has been taken to another prison inside Paris, the Conciergerie, and the young prince has been moved into solitary confinement within the Temple prison," Monsieur Tussaud reports.

"But he's so young!" I cry. "And Mama is all alone, too?"

Monsieur Tussaud looks sharply at Mademoiselle. "Mama?"

Slowly, she nods.

"Anna Marie, how . . . ? It's not possible!"

"I know you would never reveal our secret," Mademoiselle says calmly.

"Of course not — but this is lunacy! You know that, don't you? If anyone ever found out . . . they'd kill you. They'd kill you all!"

"They won't find out," Mademoiselle insists. "There's a girl in prison who looks just like her."

"You mean they'll kill her, instead?" Monsieur Tussaud says gravely.

"Perhaps they won't kill anyone else," Mademoiselle suggests.

"Perhaps not," Monsieur Tussaud agrees, his eyes on me, but I can tell he doesn't believe it.

Poor Louis-Charles! What are these monsters doing to him? He's never been separated from Mama before this. Mama must be sick with worry. And she has no one at all to comfort her.

But in the back of my mind, the worst worry of all is:

Would they really kill Ernestine in my place?

The longer my thoughts race around in my head, the worse I feel until I'm nauseated. "I have to go lie down," I say, blinking back tears and heading for the bedroom.

Crying myself to sleep, I once more dream of Brigitte lying in her case as the Belle Zulima. As I peer in at her, Brigitte changes into Mama.

Mama — lying there with her eyes closed and her face ashen. This time there's no head turn, no saucy wink.

Slowly the case fills with a white, foggy vapor that grows ever more dense until her form is almost completely obscured. Then it bursts, shattering glass everywhere.

Mama hovers in the air above the blasted coffin, radiant with an inner light. She seems confused, but then she spies me gazing up at her.

"Where must I go now, Marie-Thérèse, my Mousseline Serieuse?" she asks. "My spirit is lost. Where should it go?"

"Don't go, Mama!" I say. "Don't go anywhere. Stay here with me."

"All right," Mama agrees, but as she hovers there her form becomes like smoke and begins drifting around the room, stretching her form until it's nothing but mist.

As I reach out — to do what? Gather the light in my arms? — the vapor whirls in one direction, a spinning vortex. As it clears, a form emerges. It's Brigitte and she's inhaled all the mist into her body. "I feel quite well again," she announces with a smile.

When I awake, Brigitte is sitting up in bed. "Are you all right?" she asks. "You were crying out in your sleep."

"I'm not all right," I admit. "I'm so worried about my mother and brother that I can hardly stand it. And I had the strangest dream. I dreamt you were the Belle Zulima and you inhaled my mother's dead spirit. It cured you."

"That is strange," Brigitte says. "I don't think anything can cure me. I feel weaker every day."

"Is Rose here?" I ask. Rose is skilled at interpreting the meanings of dreams. "I want to tell her this dream and see what she thinks."

"She was in here while you were asleep and we spoke. But don't bother her now," Brigitte advises.

"Why not?"

"They've sentenced Alexandre, her husband, to be guillotined."

CHAPTER 25

That summer, my family's things are all over Paris. The revolutionaries have decided that all the items in Versailles, along with the things in the Petit Trianon, should be auctioned off to raise more money for their cause.

It's horrible to see drunken, slovenly women parading the streets wearing Mama's gowns. People push wheelbarrows through the streets of Paris that are loaded with lamps, chairs, and rugs that I recognize from my girlhood. I nearly weep when I see a man toting a box full of the locks and clocks Papa so enjoyed to tinker with.

I'm coming back from the market with my purchases when Henri calls from behind and runs to catch up with me. He's holding something behind his back. "I have something for you. Close your eyes and put out your hands."

I do as he requests, and in a minute he's placed something in my waiting hands. Opening my eyes, I gasp with delight.

It's the music box I had as a girl, the one with the shepherdess and her daughter that twirl when the music plays. "Where did you . . . ? How did you . . . ?" I stammer.

"I stole it," Henri admits proudly.

"What?"

"Well, not really," he allows. "They stole it from you, so I simply stole it back. It was in a pile of things being auctioned in the square at the Palais-Royal. I just grabbed it and ran."

I'm suddenly fearful that someone will see me with this, and I stash it in the sack with the food I just bought.

"Does, it make you sad?" Henri asks. "It didn't occur to me that it might bring back memories you don't want. I'm sorry if I —"

"No, I love it!" I interrupt. "Mama and I would dance to this tune. Those were happy times." Looping my arm through his, I begin to walk in a circle. He lets me lead him at first but then spins me. Around I go. Once, then twice.

I smile for the first time in a very long while.

I'm delighted that he knows this simple country dance I did as a younger girl out in the fields of the country retreat. Closing my eyes, I imagine myself back there.

We twirl and promenade a few more times, and then I kiss Henri on the cheek. "I love you. Thank you for getting my music box back."

"I love you, too, Ernestine Marie-Thérèse," Henri says as we walk toward the wax exhibit. I squeeze his arm, resting my head on his shoulder.

"What if you'd been caught?"

"I'm faster than any of those fat old guards," he says with a grin. "I had to get it for you so you can play the music and be happy remembering those good times."

"I used to think those times would come again, but I don't anymore," I say.

"We can't be children anymore, but we can recall how much fun it was."

Am I being what Mama used to call me: Mousseline Serieuse, *serious muslin*? Maybe I am, so I try to be a bit lighter. "You're right, Henri. We always have our memories, and no one can ever take them from us."

"I'll always remember you and it'll make me happy," Henri says.

I stop walking, turning to face him. "You won't have to remember me, Henri, because we'll always be together."

"You're not being realistic," Henri says, stepping away to face me.

"I am," I insist. Yet despite my words, it occurs to me that maybe he's right. What if I go back to being royal? Suddenly, I don't want that.

I'm so divided! I want the Revolution to fail for the sake of my family. I love them so much. If the Revolution fails, I will see them again.

At the same time, although I despise its brutality, if the Revolution means the people won't be so poor — I want that, too. Liberty and fraternity. Freedom and brotherhood. Those are the virtues the Revolution espouses, and I believe in those things, as well.

I want it all! I want my family *and* Henri.

"Maybe things will be different someday soon," Henri says, taking my hand.

"I see no sign that the Revolution is going to stop," I say, which is true.

"I wouldn't be so certain," Henri disagrees. "There's talk of war everywhere. Foreign armies are at our borders. The monarchy has royal friends and even family who might invade at any time. We've been at war with Prussia, Hungary, and Bohemia. Just last February, we declared war on England and Holland."

"But it all seems so far away," I say.

"The fighting could come closer. There's talk of war with Austria, too," Henri adds.

Why haven't my Austrian uncles come to Mama's aid? She also has sisters who've married the heads of other countries. Why haven't they helped her?

Yet this idea that invading armies might free what's left of my family fills me with hope. No matter what happens, I'll find a way to stay with Henri. I've read of Queen Elizabeth of England who refused to marry. That's what I'll do, but secretly we'll wed.

All at once, a sunniness envelops me that I haven't felt in a very long time. We're near a park whose gardens are still beautiful, even though they've fallen into disrepair. Grabbing Henri's hand, I pull him off the street and into the park. There, I wind the music box and set it on a bench. Stepping close, I take hold of him and we dance to the happy melody.

How very handsome Henri is, especially when he smiles at me, as he's doing now.

*   *   *

Fall comes and the weather grows dank. Our moods mirror the season, but it's not only the outside climate that's responsible. Mademoiselle's Monsieur Tussaud has taken a trip to England. He claims he's looking for a place for them to live when the time is right, but I believe Mademoiselle worries that he's not coming back.

Rose's husband is still awaiting execution, and Rose is starting to suspect that the general is exerting his influence to keep Alexandre de Beauharnais imprisoned because he wants Rose — or Joséphine, as he likes to call her — for himself.

The dismal gray autumn weather has hit Brigitte the hardest. She's picked up a hacking cough and seems weaker every day. It's difficult for me and Henri to sleep with Brigitte tossing and coughing through the night. This sleeplessness makes us tired and irritable in the daytime.

And the beheadings continue relentlessly. Day in and day out, droves of people lose their heads at the Place de la Révolution. Every day we come home, spattered in blood, carrying our baskets filled with the wide-eyed visages of the newly decapitated. At least in the colder weather, the flies don't swarm around them as much.

Only Henri keeps a bright demeanor. "How do you stay so cheerful?" I whine at him one day when I've had my fill of even his smile.

"I don't think, I just do. If I began to brood, I might never stop, so I don't allow myself to begin." I wonder if he's the most sensitive of us all, that he must build such a wall around his thoughts. I don't think I could be like him, though. It's just not in me.

And so we go on this way. Then comes a day that's etched in my head forever — the most horrible day of my life.

It's October 16, and we head toward the Place de la Révolution for our usual grizzly task. The crowd is somehow more agitated than usual, but I can't find anyone to tell me why.

Leaving Mademoiselle and Henri, I try to find a newspaper seller and see one at the end of the boulevard. Before I can reach him, though, a roar of raised voices swells around me as a tumbrel of prisoners comes around the corner.

Shouting, the mob rushes forward but is held back by guards with their guns.

I climb onto a park wall to get a better view. What could be agitating them so?

The horse-drawn cart contains only women prisoners. At first I don't see anyone I recognize. Then I look again and freeze at the sight before me.

Mama is in the tumbrel.

She's dressed in a plain white muslin gown. Her hair has been chopped very short and is covered by a ruffled cap. She's pale but dignified as the awful mob jeers and insults her.

"Citizen Marie Capet to die today!" a newsboy shouts, hawking his paper.

"Mama!" I shout at the top of my voice, not caring who might realize my identity. I'm beyond caring. I wave my arms wildly for her attention. "Mama! Mama!"

She's heard me! I see her searching the crowd.

"Mama! Here!" Some turn toward me, but then look away, disinterested in a lunatic girl.

"Mama!"

At last, we connect. Her hands cover her face as tears finally spill down her cheeks.

I am dissolved in my own grief, drowning in rivers of sorrow. "Mama!" I croak with outstretched arms.

With a small movement, Mama shakes her head and dashes the wetness from her face. I know what she's telling me: *You're making a scene. You must stop. Don't let them find you.*

The tumbrel is moving on and I try to follow, but the crowd is thick and won't let me pass. What should I do now? Maybe I should go and be with her when the end comes.

Oh, I can't!

To see Mama die would be too horrible. And perhaps it would be worse for her to have me there. I remember how Papa didn't come see us the morning of his execution. Mama explained to us later that the sadness would have been unbearable, and he couldn't have gone to his death with dignity, as he did, if he'd seen us that morning.

I'm suddenly dizzy and I stumble, falling from the low wall. My head bangs against it as I topple, my head crashing a second time onto the sidewalk.

No one stops to help me or even to inquire if I'm hurt.

Head down and sick to the pit of my stomach, I drag myself back to the wax exhibit and go to my bedroom. Usually when I enter, Brigitte stirs in her sleep, but this time she doesn't. Her exquisite face is so pale it looks like one of Mademoiselle's wax faces before she applies the paint.

Laying my hand on her cheek, I immediately feel that it's like ice.

Brigitte is dead.

Strangely, I feel nothing other than an overwhelming fatigue, and I curl up at the end of Brigitte's bed. My head pounds as though someone were slamming my skull with a club.

A surge of nausea hits me, and I vomit from the side of the bed. That helps lessen the knot in my gut and the torture in my head — but only slightly.

Finally, I tumble into a deep hole of slumber that's so deep not even dreams can find me. My pain is gone in this place, and I hope I can stay there forever. It's very peaceful.

Sometimes I hear a murmur of voices, but I'm too far away to reply to them. I don't want to be rescued. I like where I am. It's safe from violence, cruelty, loss, and grief.

After a while, I don't hear these voices anymore.

CHAPTER 26

*M*y secret hiding place deep within myself becomes the gardens of Versailles, the Petit Trianon. In this dream state there is sunshine, music, and birds. For a long time I sit on a bench where I watch the sparkling fountains of the palace grounds shimmer in the light. Resting like this makes me grow stronger.

After a while, I feel lonely. I especially long to see Henri.

Then one day, I awake. I'm lying in the bed that once was mine before Brigitte occupied it.

An elderly man with white hair wipes my forehead with a warm, wet rag. "You've come back to us," he says. I've seen him before, but I can't remember where.

Opening my mouth to speak, I'm speechless. The man lifts my head in order to spoon some water into my mouth. "Rest," he advises in a kindly tone. "You've been in a comatose state for a long time, many months. Don't try to talk. I'll tell you what's been happening."

He calls a name and a woman comes into the room. I've seen her, too, but am unsure why I recognize her. She has a pile of unruly black hair and is dressed as a gypsy. She beams happily when she sees that I'm awake. The man asks her to bring me some broth, and she departs quickly to get it.

"I am Dr. Curtius and that woman is Madame Grosholtz. You know her daughter, Anna Marie."

Dr. Curtius, of course! And Mademoiselle's mother. I recall her taking money at the door of the exhibit. It's like remembering another life.

"The revolutionary government threatened to arrest Anna Marie once more. We heard they were coming for her, so she secretly married Monsieur Tussaud and they left for London. She hated to leave you, but I assured her I would care for you."

"Thank you." This time my voice is a croaking whisper, but at least it works.

"Rose wasn't as lucky. She's in prison once more," Dr. Curtius continues.

"Henri?" I ask.

"In prison, also. They accused him of helping Anna Marie escape, which he did. They say that makes him an enemy of France."

My poor Henri!

"Marie-Thérèse-Charlotte?" I ask, not sure if he knows who I really am.

"Your double is still in the Temple prison, as is your unfortunate brother, Louis-Charles."

"Aunt Élisabeth?" I ask.

"I don't know." Something in his expression, maybe the way he averts his eyes, tells me he does know. I'm convinced she's been beheaded. All this bad news is too much. Closing my eyes, I feel the secret hiding place deep within me calling for my return.

But Dr. Curtius shakes my arm, keeping me tethered to the present. "Stay with us, Marie-Thérèse. There's hope yet."

Madame Grosholtz returns with the broth, which she gingerly feeds me as Dr. Curtius continues, "Robespierre angered the Committee of Public Safety and has been beheaded. The Committee is trying to distance itself from the atrocities of the Terror. It will please you to know that they're even improving the conditions of the children who remain in the Temple prison."

I nod. "Thank God."

"The Committee cares about how France looks in the eyes of the world. They're ashamed of much of what's happened in the name of liberty."

"As well they should be," Madame Grosholtz grumbles.

"Will they release Rose and Henri?" I ask hopefully.

"I don't know," Dr. Curtius replies. "So many prisoners still die each day."

My stomach lurches and I wave the bowl away. Turning on my side, I return to the blessed oblivion of sleep.

This time, though, it takes only forty-eight hours before I awaken again. My voice returns to its original strength. Each day, I eat and my body regains some strength. After two weeks of recovery, I stand, taking shaky steps at first but gradually growing steadier. In a month I'm nearly fully recovered.

Dr. Curtius and Madame Grosholtz are so kind to me. They seem like an old married couple, though I can't figure out the exact nature of their relationship.

My blonde hair has grown back to its original length and color. Madame Grosholtz combs brown dye through it and plaits it down my back.

I begin working at the wax exhibit again, helping Dr. Curtius with the figures and guiding tours. No longer do I go collect the heads of the newly murdered. For some reason, the government doesn't press Dr. Curtius to do this. Maybe they have more wax faces than they know what to do with. It could be that they now want to hide the evidence of their murders. Whatever the reason, I'm overwhelmingly relieved to be free of this hideous task at last.

One day in June, Madame Grosholtz finds me in the work studio and says she must tell me something important. Her grim expression frightens me. She takes my hand and guides me to a bench, where we both sit. "Your brother passed away today," she reveals. "He was sick in the prison, and there was nothing anyone could do."

Little Louis-Charles! What have they done to him?

I thank Madame and wait until she's gone before I let my tears flow. My dear brother, the sweetest little boy in the world. How much more can I stand? Will this trail of misery and loss ever end?

$\mathcal{C}$HAPTER 27

$\mathcal{B}$ut I do bear more — six months more of dull days. I couldn't understand why I should be alive when Papa, Mama, and Louis-Charles were not. One day in December, I am headed across rue Saint-Honoré when I see a coach pull up in front of a grand restaurant a few paces ahead of me. To my delight, Rose steps out of the coach. She sees me and her face lights up.

"Rose! You're free!" I cry out and hurry toward her.

She's never looked more regal, with her dark curls bundled to the top of her head, encircled in a wide golden band. Her high-waist gown is the very latest fashion, as is the satin-lined cloak draped over her shoulders. On her hand is a dazzling sapphire and diamond ring.

In the next moment, General Bonaparte steps out of the carriage behind her, his face haughty, and I decide I don't care for him very much.

"Don't let her call you Rose," General Bonaparte commands Rose sharply. "From now on, you will be known only as Joséphine Bonaparte."

Rose glances at him but makes no reply as she bends to embrace me. "Ah, my dear girl," she says quietly. "I'm so glad to see you up and well. You had us all so frightened." She turns to the general. "You remember my friend Ernestine, do you not? We drove her home in your carriage that night."

"Yes, of course," General Bonaparte agrees, clearly disinterested.

"How have you been, Ernestine?" Rose asks.

"Dr. Curtius and Madame Grosholtz treat me well," I assure her. "Is Henri free, also?"

"As far as I know, he's still in prison. They freed me five days after they beheaded my husband. But they're letting people go free every day. He might be out anytime now."

Bending my head, I lower my voice. "Do you hear anything of the fate of the royal children?"

"They've allowed the princess to stroll in the Temple garden lately, something they haven't done before," Rose confides. "I haven't seen the little prince, though. I'm afraid he might be . . . very ill."

"He's died," I tell her.

Rose presses me into a tight hug. "I'm so very sorry, chérie."

General Bonaparte coughs impatiently.

Rose hugs me once more. "Listen to me carefully now," she whispers, still keeping me enclosed in her embrace. "It's fate that we've run into each other. Anna Marie left you a note in the lining of your little music box."

"What does it say?"

Rose shakes her head. "Read it. Be sure you read it when you're alone." She gazes deeply, pointedly, into my eyes. "No one else can see it."

The general coughs once more.

"Forgive me, my sweet," Rose apologizes, cupping General Bonaparte's pointed chin tenderly. "Farewell, Ernestine. Remember what I've told you. Be well until we meet again."

"Until we meet again," I echo as General Bonaparte takes her arm and escorts her into the restaurant.

I can't work now — I'm too excited. I have to see what the note tucked in my music box tells me.

But I also need to see Ernestine, and so I head toward rue du Temple. A small crowd has gathered at the perimeter of the castle, and this makes me hopeful that someone is outdoors. The people seem calm now, not as wildly vengeful as before, more curious than spiteful.

Squeezing to the front of the crowd, I peer through the spiked iron fence to see Ernestine pacing, rubbing her arms to keep warm. How pale and painfully thin she's become! Her expression is so profoundly sad. And she has neither a cloak, nor gloves, not even a warm hat. How she must long for fresh air to be willing to come out, even in this cold.

"Citizen Marie Capet!" I shout, calling her by the name that all the newspapers use when referring to her, to me.

I hope she recognizes my voice, and she does. She walks straight for me, and the crowd is riveted.

"You're just a chink in the wall," I say angrily to her.

"A chink in the wall? How dare you?" she responds.

"Yes, just a chink in the wall."

I back away, hoping she understands. Some of the crowd cheer me because they think I've insulted the arrogant princess, but others scowl at me. They seem to feel she's suffered enough.

It seems to take forever to run around the streets to rue de Beaujolais where the park area is by the back wall. Thankfully, no one is around on such a frigid day. Ernestine is already there when I arrive.

"I'm so happy you came," she says, mist coming from her lips. "I think they're going to let me out tomorrow."

"How wonderful!" I reply. "What time will that happen?"

"I don't know. At dawn, I think, maybe before. We're to slip out of Paris as unnoticed as possible. They're going to disguise us."

"I wish we knew exactly when."

"Come while it's still dark to be safe. You have to be here. The Holy Roman Emperor, Francis the Second, has personally requested that Marie-Thérèse-Charlotte's playmate, Ernestine, be allowed to travel to Austria with her. No one knows where she is, but if you show up, I'm sure they'll take you. It's our chance for the both of us to escape together."

"They're sending you — us — to Austria?" I ask.

"Yes. Vienna. Your mother's family has agreed to take us in."

"Tell them you've received word that I'll be there. Then, in the coach, I'll switch clothing with you and go back to being me."

"But your hair! How will you explain that?" Ernestine asks in a panicked voice.

"I'll get a wig from one of the exhibits."

"Yes, that's good. I hope Louis-Charles comes with us," Ernestine says. "Perhaps your mother and Aunt Élisabeth will come, also."

The mention of Mama, Louis-Charles, and Aunt Élisabeth makes me so lonely. Clearly, Ernestine does not know anything of the outside world. I decide not to tell her. I don't want to talk about their deaths, and she'll find out soon enough.

"I can't believe I'm really going to be free. And we'll be together again!" Ernestine's teeth chatter with the cold, but she's so happy.

"We will! But now I have to go. I'll be back tomorrow."

"Come to rue Meslay during the early hours of the morning. I couldn't stand it if we had to leave without you."

"I'll be there."

"Until tomorrow," she says, leaving the wall.

I fold my arms for warmth as I head back to the exhibit. My head spins with this new information. It's so sudden — so unexpected. How can I leave while Henri is still imprisoned? My family is all gone now. If it weren't for Henri, there would be nothing to hold me here.

But Henri *is* here, and I can't leave him.

And yet . . . I have family in Austria — aunts, uncles, grandparents. They want to help me. It's the opportunity I've been hoping for.

Is there more hope of freeing Henri if I go to my family? If I stay behind, I'm powerless to do anything. If I go . . . maybe there's a chance I could inspire them to return to Paris and free those in the jails.

I don't know! I think the smart thing to do is to leave while I have the chance. If anyone were to discover my true identity, I might also be a victim of the guillotine. Once they realize Ernestine is gone, the revolutionaries might search for her in the streets.

I decide I must go, and so I return to the exhibit to pack my things and tell Dr. Curtius and Madame Grosholtz that I'll be leaving. And most important, I have to see what's in the note Mademoiselle has left for me.

When I come into the exhibit, though, Dr. Curtius and Madame Grosholtz are in another room with paperwork laid out on the table in front of them and it doesn't seem like the right time to disturb them.

I head for my bedroom, looking it over. I've lived here for over two years. It's hard to believe I'll really be leaving. Henri's empty bed is still on the other side of the hung sheet, though it has been stripped of its bedding.

My music box has sat unopened for months. I haven't looked at it or listened to its sweet folk song since before I fell into my deep sleep. Now I sit on my bed and open it. The music instantly begins. The mother and daughter shepherdesses twirl.

I wiggle my finger into the seams of the pink satin that lines the box. Frustrated, I turn the box upside down. There's nothing on the bottom and no letter spills out. I assumed I'd find it right away, so I didn't ask Rose to be more exact.

When I set it right again, I notice that the little oval mirror glued to the inside cover of the box, behind the spinning figures, is slightly out of place. Excitedly, I pry the mirror off and there it is — a folded note glued under the mirror.

I open it, my hands shaking.

Marie-Thérèse, I know that someday you will wake up. You're a strong girl and this sleeping, though understandable, will not go on forever. While you slept, Rose and I have worked feverishly on our "experiments." With one experiment we had lucky timing and it might have worked, though we can't be sure of how long the effect will last. You must find your way to a farm owned by a family named LeFleur outside the village of Charenton. If the meaning of this letter does not become clear to you, then it's safe to say that we failed once more. It has been my honor to know you. Until we meet again. Madame Anna Marie Tussaud.

What is she saying? What have they done?

Do I dare to hope any one of my family has been brought back from their awful death? Is it even possible?

The idea is so shocking — so overpowering — that I can't think straight. Stunned, I sit on my bed, clutching the note, unable to put together a sensible idea or thought or plan.

But slowly another consideration occurs to me.

How am I to do this if I must leave for Vienna tomorrow?

My head spins with uncertainty. What is the right thing to do? I have no idea.

CHAPTER 28

*T*hat evening, I speak to Dr. Curtius and Madame Grosholtz, though I don't say anything about the note, since I promised Rose I wouldn't. They both agree that I must go with Ernestine in the morning. "It's the only way you'll ever be assured of your safety or will regain the security of your family."

"They're not really my family," I argue. "I've never met most of them. Even the uncles who've visited I hardly recall."

"You're a Hapsburg princess, and that will mean a lot to them. Under their protection, you'll marry a royal and live the life you were born to, a royal life," Dr. Curtius insists.

How strange that idea seems now, after all that's happened. I can't even picture myself leading such a life anymore. In fact, I don't even want it. It's so unfair. How can I live so lavishly now that I've seen how most people struggle just to survive? I'd never feel good about the luxury and wealth again.

I would like the security, though, and the sense of family.

Later that night, I pack a few things, my music box among them, the only remains of my former life. I can hardly sleep for anticipating the coming day's events. It's almost midnight and I can't stand it any longer.

Instantly, I'm up and making my way through the dark wax museum. I'm glad I said my good-byes earlier. I understand now how hard it is to say farewell when you know you might never return. Wrapping my wool shawl around my shoulders, I open the exhibit door for the last time.

It's a strange sensation to be out on the dark streets of Paris when they're so empty. The only sounds are the cooing of the mourning doves and the rattle of the winter wind. Trash blows past me as I hurry along toward the Temple prison.

Despite the early hour, I'm late for my appointment. "Here's Ernestine!" I hear Ernestine say in a loud voice to some people standing near a horse-drawn coach, and I start to run.

"Hurry," says a woman I've never seen before. We dash inside the carriage, and the driver, a soldier named Mechin, takes his place. We ride with a prison guard named Gomin; a plump, older woman named Madame de Soucy; and her maid.

As we ride out of Paris, we hear the church bells chime twelve. "I've been in prison for three years, four months, and five days," Ernestine says, and tears spring to her eyes.

"Well, you are free now," says Madame de Soucy.

"Not yet," says Gomin. "There are many who would still like to capture or even kill you, Princess. If we're stopped, they might well kill us all."

Madame de Soucy makes a snort of disapproval, scowling deeply at the guard.

"It's simply true, Madame," he defends himself. "We won't be safe until we are over the border."

One by one, the adults are lulled to sleep by the steady rocking of the carriage.

"I wonder how soon until you'll wed Antoine," Ernestine says with a wistful tone.

"I wish you could marry him instead."

"So do I," Ernestine says. "We got on so well. I've never forgotten him. Since the day we first met, he's always been on my mind."

That's how I feel about Henri. It's as though we've melded into one being. What affects him also affects me, and I believe it's the same for him with me. Could Ernestine and Antoine have made that same kind of connection? Can love at first sight really exist? Perhaps it can. It could be that deep down a person recognizes a perfect mate instantly.

Ernestine has been through so much because of me: falling in love with a young man she can never have is probably as bad as all she's endured in prison.

"I'm so sorry you had to suffer in my place," I say.

"It was terrible," Ernestine tells me, "but I've done it for so long that it will be difficult to go back to not being a princess."

"I'd gladly let you take over for me."

"No, you wouldn't. Not now. The horrible years are over. Now everything will be grand balls and sumptuous dinners and beautiful clothing once more."

"I don't want that," I insist. I gaze at Ernestine, my dear childhood friend. "Would you really like to go on being me?" I ask.

A seed of hope has sprung to life within me.

"I would love it," she says, "but, of course, that can't ever be."

The carriage rolls to a stop and for a long moment Ernestine and I grip each other's hands. What's happening?

There's a quick rap from outside the curtained carriage window. Pushing aside the curtain, I see it's Mechin. "Don't be alarmed. I'm just stopping here at Charenton to water the horses. We'll be going again in a moment."

Thanking him, I lean back in my seat.

Then, with a jolt, I realize what he's just said.

Charenton! We've stopped in Charenton!

It's the village that Mademoiselle Grosholtz told me to find.

Fate has brought me here.

And suddenly, I know what I must do. I embrace Ernestine in a sharp, quick hug. "I'm going, Ernestine," I whisper. "You will be princess. Never tell anyone that you're not."

"Are you mad?" Ernestine asks in alarm. "Where will you go?"

"I'm not sure. Say you were asleep, and when you awoke I was gone. Maybe I went out to relieve myself and was left behind. Perhaps I ran away. It doesn't matter. You're the important one. They won't go back for me. And if they do, they won't find me."

Ernestine grabs my arm. "Where will you live?"

"I'm not sure. You go and enjoy being a princess. I know you'll continue to be wonderful at it."

Madame de Soucy stirs in her sleep. She opens her eyes, readjusts her position, and then drifts off once more.

Outside, a horse whinnies, reminding me that I have only a short while to make my escape.

Hugging Ernestine once more, I crack open the carriage door and check that there is no one around. Blowing a kiss, I grab my bag, pull my shawl around my shoulders, and slide out of the carriage. "Until we meet again, dear friend," I whisper.

In the distance, I see Mechin walking back toward the coach. I inch around the back and stealthily slide into the darkest part of the road until I find the cover of some thick bushes. Panting with excitement, I crouch there until the carriage rides away, watching it recede into the distance.

Slowly, I stand and survey my surroundings. The moon has risen high in the night sky and lights my way. The wind shakes the foliage, making me shiver. There's a barn just across a field. Letting myself in, I spend the hours until dawn buried under a pile of hay inside its walls. When the brightening sky breaks through the barn's wooden slats, I struggle out of the hay, brush my clothing, and set out walking down the road in search of the LeFleur farm.

CHAPTER 29

The man on horseback of whom I ask directions knows of the LeFleur farm, so it's not difficult to find, though it's about five miles away. With my bag slung over my shoulder, I head toward it, walking quickly on the road between yellow-brown fields lying dormant for the winter. Occasionally, I see sheep and goats nibbling on hay that someone has laid out for them. The bleating of the sheep makes me think of how Mama and I would play at being shepherdesses in our field.

When I arrive at the LeFleur farm, I'm charmed by the sign on the gate, a plainly rendered painting of violets and the name of the farm. How simple and pretty it is. The stone house beyond the wooden gate is equally cozy and welcoming.

But now what do I do? I don't truly know what I'm searching for. If anyone were to ask me, what would I say? I've been told to come here, but I don't know why.

Heading up the wide lane toward the house, I decide to ask for employment. That will at least get me through the door. After that, I'll see whatever there is to see.

Nervously, I step onto the front porch and rap on the door, my heart hammering.

A plump, white-haired woman in a plain, apron-covered dress answers the door when I knock. "Excuse me," I say, "I'm hoping you might have a job for me."

The woman looks me over and her expression is kind. "What kind of work do you want?"

"I'll do anything. I can read and write. I've worked as an artist's assistant. I can clean. I'm a quick learner."

A soft smile appears on the woman's face. She opens the door wider and gestures for me to enter. "We need help in the kitchen making the jellies and jams. You'll also have to help with the pickling and canning, which should be complete by now but isn't."

"I can do that."

"Do you mind goats and sheep?"

"I love them."

This makes her laugh. "What's your name?"

How do I answer that? I don't want to say Ernestine de Lambriquet. What if someone comes looking for me? "Anna Marie Grosholtz," I say.

"You're from Alsace?" the woman asks.

"My grandfather was," I say, thinking of Dr. Curtius. "I've always lived in Paris."

A suspicious expression appears on the woman's face. "Why are you so far from home? How did you get here?"

This time I tell the truth. "My parents and other relatives were guillotined for unintentionally angering the revolutionaries. My brothers and sisters have all died from sickness. I have no family left, and my friends have fled or been imprisoned. I'm on my own and want a safer life in the country."

Suspicion has softened into sympathy, and the woman puts her arm around me. "If you're a good worker, you'll have a place here. The LeFleurs are kind, honest people. I've worked for them since I was a girl your age. My name is Celeste."

In the kitchen, two cooks, one tall and older, the other petite and about twenty, work at the large stove, stirring big pots. The wooden table is laden with apples, carrots, and potatoes. "Here are Sophie and Monique," Celeste tells me, then turns to the cooks. "Anna Marie will be helping you."

I scrutinize the women. Were they perhaps servants back at Versailles? But I'm sure I don't know them, nor do they give any indication that they recognize me.

"Welcome, Anna Marie," says the taller woman, Sophie. "We need your help. Those apples won't be crisp for much longer if we don't use them."

Monique hands me an apron and a paring knife. "Start with the apples and then peel the potatoes." She sees my hesitation and adds, "This knife is tricky. I'll show you how I like to do it."

"Thank you," I say, grateful for her help. I sit on a stool at the table and discover that it's not really difficult to peel an apple or a potato.

Before long I'm slicing them and the kitchen fills with mouth-watering aromas as the maids bake apple pies and make applesauce. "The Christmas meal has to be readied," Sophie explains. "Then we'll start canning."

After several hours of peeling, chopping, and baking, Monique places a slice of apple pie by my side. "Take this upstairs to the governess. The children nap at this hour, and I usually like to send her a snack. You'll find her room at the top of the stairs."

I take the pie and climb the stairs. The door of the top room is ajar and a blonde woman sits with her back to me, writing at a desk. "I have a pie for you, Madame," I say.

Slowly, the woman turns. Her expression is friendly at first but immediately becomes wide-eyed with surprise.

I freeze in place, shocked, and she knocks over her bottle of ink as she stands.

It's Brigitte — the beautiful Belle Zulima!

Alive!

"Brig —"

"My Mousseline Serieuse!"

The plate I'm holding crashes to the floor.

"Mama?" I ask, trembling.

Her arms open wide to embrace me, and she takes a halting step forward. "Yes! Yes! My child! My angel! It is I."

And I know deep in my heart that it is.

"Mama!" I cry as we fall into each other's arms. We hug and weep, laugh and smile, until we're exhausted.

"How, Mama? How can this be?" I finally ask.

Mama shuts the door, guiding me to a small couch, where we sit. "It's all very strange to me. Listen. After my execution, my spirit hovered over my body, not quite believing that I was dead. I had to see my children one last time. As soon as I thought it, I was transported back to the Temple prison, where I hugged Louis-Charles, so sick, so mistreated."

"I'm sure he was comforted even if he didn't know why," I say. "He's died, you know."

"I didn't know," Mama replies, her voice cracking once more. "How they tortured him," she adds, shaking her head. "At least he's free of them, at last."

"What happened after you left Louis-Charles?" I ask.

"Then I longed to see you, so I traveled to where you were sleeping so deeply that I was certain you had died. It grieved me so much that I longed to be taken from this world at last. I heard female voices calling me to them. I thought they were angels summoning me to heaven, and so I gladly went."

"Mademoiselle and Rose . . ." I realize breathlessly.

"When I traveled toward the voices, I found they were two women in a workroom, and a woman was lying on the table." She points to herself. "She was the woman whose body I now inhabit."

"Brigitte," I tell her. "She died on the same day you did."

"The women said words in some strange tongue, words that lulled me into a trance. When I awoke, I was looking out of the eyes of this lovely woman. I've been alive in her body ever since."

Once more, I fall into her arms, so overwhelmingly grateful for this miracle.

$\mathscr{C}$HAPTER 30

We tell people we're sisters, since Mama now looks too young to be my mother. I call her Antonia and she refers to me as Anna Marie. Our story is that we were separated because of the Revolution but have been searching for each other. Everyone can feel our joy at being reunited.

"How did you get here?" I ask her the next day as I feed the goats in their pen and Mama watches the two small LeFleur children, a girl and a boy, run in the adjacent field.

"When I realized I was still alive, I remembered this farm and the sweet sign in front. I'd passed it as a young girl on my way to the French palace where I was groomed to become a queen. I never forgot the lovely simplicity of it."

"You told Mademoiselle Grosholtz?"

"Yes. After she left, I walked for many weeks, sleeping in barns and on the side of the road. I was half starved by the time I reached the front gate. I collapsed right at the sign, but the LeFleurs found me and nursed me to health. Then, when they discovered I could read, write, and speak several languages, they engaged me as a governess for their children. I'm so happy here. LeFleur farm is the place I was hoping to re-create at the Petit Trianon."

"This is the model for our country home?" I ask, amazed.

"Yes, and now we've found our way here, to the real place of my dreams."

It's strange how a life I once would've considered boring now seems wonderfully tranquil and safe. Perhaps I've grown old beyond my years.

I long for news of my friends, but it's hard to come by. One day, Sophie comes back from a trip into the village of Charenton with a newspaper. "Marie-Thérèse-Charlotte has married the duc d'Angoulême," she says casually, tossing the paper on a side table. "I hope that poor girl finds some happiness at last after all she's suffered."

Smiling, I inspect the paper and see a drawing of Ernestine in a lovely wedding dress standing beside Antoine. In the picture they both seem radiant with happiness. But then I feel a pang. What's happened to Henri? Will I ever see him again?

And then one day, a young man comes to the door. I'm at the top of the stairs, and I hear him talking to Celeste at the front door.

I know his voice instantly.

In the next moment, I'm thundering down the stairs. "Henri!" I cry joyfully, hurtling into his arms. We stumble backward onto the porch, kissing, ecstatic to be reunited.

"How did you find me?" I ask between passionate kisses.

"I contacted Madame Tussaud when they released me from prison," Henri explains.

Concerned, I look into his face. He's thinner and appears older than he should for nineteen. Wrapping my arms around him, I rest my cheek on his chest, listening to his heartbeat. "Everything's all right now," I say. "Nothing can ever part us again."

And nothing ever does.

$\mathcal{A}$UTHOR'S $\mathcal{N}$OTE

Obviously, this is a work of fiction, but I've tried my best to stay true to the main events of the French Revolution. The place where I've taken the greatest liberty is in the age of Marie-Thérèse. For most of her sixteenth and seventeenth years, she sat in one of several jails, completely alone toward the end. So, in the interest of a better story, one that didn't read like a textbook on the French Revolution, I've made her character older than she actually was at the start of the Revolution.

Marie-Thérèse-Charlotte was the only member of her immediate family to survive the Revolution and really was released from the Temple prison at midnight on her seventeenth birthday in 1795. Frances II of Austria wrote to the French Minister of the Interior requesting that Ernestine de Lambriquet accompany the princess to Austria. He was told that the girl had gone into hiding and couldn't be found. We know now that Ernestine was hiding with a family named Mackau from the date of the invasion of Tuileries Palace in 1792.

It is still unknown whether Ernestine did, in fact, leave Paris with the princess that night. Madame de Soucy was said to have been traveling with her teenaged son, but she never had a son, leading some to speculate that Ernestine left disguised as a boy.

We know that Ernestine de Lambriquet was a girl who looked very much like the princess and who was the daughter of a palace chambermaid. In 1788, Louis XVI established a substantial allowance for Ernestine (12,000 livres). It was rumored that Ernestine might also have been another child of Louis XVI from the maid Philippine de Lambriquet. Throughout the years there has been a lot of conjecture as to whether Princess Marie-Thérèse changed places with Ernestine at the time of her release. Later portraits suggest differences in the princesses' noses, which those who believe she was really Ernestine often point to as proof. Those who don't believe it claim that Ernestine went to London and lived an ordinary, peaceful life. This novel embraces the idea that Ernestine de Lambriquet spent the rest of her life acting as Marie-Thérèse-Charlotte. Almost immediately upon her marriage to the duc d'Angoulême people noted that she seemed different in manner and appearance from Marie-Thérèse-Charlotte. We know Marie-Thérèse-Charlotte was involved in various unsuccessful attempts to retake the throne. Rumors of the Dark Countess refer to a veiled woman named Sophie Botta who arrived in Hildburghausen, Germany, in 1807, with a male companion. The two seldom went out, and when they did, the woman was always veiled. People began referring to her as the Dark Countess.

Upon her death in 1837, the Dark Countess was quickly buried, but objects known to have belonged to the Bourbons and bearing the royal fleur-de-lis symbol were discovered among her possessions. The body was exhumed in October of 2013 for DNA testing in order to determine whether the woman buried there was indeed Marie-Thérèse-Charlotte de Bourbon. The body was reburied but without comment on what that testing might — or might not — have revealed. As of this writing (March 2014), the German government has once again exhumed the body for further testing to discover once and for all, through genetic testing, if this was Marie-Thérèse. (For an Internet search of this subject, try The Dark Countess, The Dailymail.co.uk, and Telegraph.co.uk) One also must question why DNA analysis is not done on the person bearing the title of Marie-Thérèse-Charlotte who is buried in the Bourbon burial crypt in Slovenia.

Other poetic license taken is in the details of Anna Marie Grosholtz, later to become known as Madame Tussaud, and of Rose de Beauharnais, who would later be Empress Joséphine Bonaparte.

Here's what is true. Joséphine Bonaparte (then called Rose de Beauharnais) was a beautiful Creole woman from Martinique who was imprisoned by the French revolutionaries because of her first marriage to the aristocrat Alexandre de Beauharnais. While in prison, she met Madame Tussaud (then named Anna Marie Grosholtz), who had been jailed by the Revolutionary Guard because she gave wax-work lessons to Princess Élisabeth, the sister of Louis XVI, the king of France, at Versailles. Since she had access to the royal family, she was accused of spying for them.

Also true is that Anna Marie Grosholtz was a student of famed waxworker Dr. Philippe Curtius — whom she called Uncle Philippe. She was released from prison, thanks to the influential friends of Dr. Curtius, just days before her execution date (her head had already been shaven) on the condition that she use her skills in waxwork to make death masks for the revolutionaries. Reluctantly, she made masks from the severed heads of Louis XVI, Marie-Antoinette, Robespierre, and Marat, among many others. (The last two happened later during the Reign of Terror.) However, unlike in this novel, Madame Tussaud didn't leave for England with her new husband until 1802.

I've moved up the time frame in the case of Rose and Napoléon Bonaparte, as well. Rose de Beauharnais was released from jail five days after the beheading of Robespierre in July 1794, which is why I had her go back to jail at that time. In reality, Rose didn't become involved with Napoléon until 1795. Up until then, she was known as Rose, but he insisted on calling her Joséphine, which she used from then on. (Josèphe was part of her name.) She married Napoléon in 1796 and became the first Empress of France in 1804. She was popular for her kindness, especially to orphans. They later divorced, mainly because Napoléon wanted a male heir, which Joséphine failed to produce.

Henri is the only main character in this novel who is wholly fictional, though he's based on the many impoverished young men and women who existed in Paris at the time. His story is based on true accounts of the lives of farmers at the time.

The character of Brigitte is also my creation, but there was, in fact, an exhibit in Paris in those years known as *The Belle Zulima*, in which a woman renowned for her beauty pretended to be a two-hundred-year-old corpse untouched by any decay and lay on display in a glass case.

Suzanne Weyn is the acclaimed author of *Dr. Frankenstein's Daughters*, *Invisible World*, *Empty*, *Distant Waves*, and *Reincarnation*, as well as *The Bar Code Tattoo*, *The Bar Code Rebellion*, and *The Bar Code Prophecy*. She lives in the middle of horse country in New York State, and can be found online at www.suzanneweynbooks.com.